Norton Powlett

Eastern legends and stories

In English verse

Norton Powlett

Eastern legends and stories
In English verse

ISBN/EAN: 9783337152604

Printed in Europe, USA, Canada, Australia, Japan

Cover: Foto ©Andreas Hilbeck / pixelio.de

More available books at **www.hansebooks.com**

EASTERN LEGENDS AND STORIES

IN ENGLISH VERSE

BY

LIEUT. NORTON POWLETT

ROYAL ARTILLERY

LONDON

HENRY S. KING & Co.

65 CORNHILL & 12 PATERNOSTER ROW

1873

PREFACE.

—◆—

THE AUTHOR, in submitting to the Public the following collection of Translations from Eastern sources, has thought it best to convert for the most part the Oriental forms of speech, which the characters in these Legends would use, into, as far as may be, their English equivalents; that what is said might sound more real in Western ears. He has reduced the number of foot-notes to the narrowest possible limits, believing that in a work of light poetry the constant intervention of notes becomes tiresome to the reader. Many, in reading this small collection of Legends, will doubtless recognize some 'Old Friends with New Faces.'

The Author can but say that they are not merely dressed up for the occasion, but that the originals have been met with by him in Eastern literature, their presence in which may be an interesting fact to the philologist, as it only adds another link to the chain of evidence that demonstrates that in the Fables and Proverbs (which are but condensed fables) of all countries, the same ideas, and frequently the same way of expressing these ideas, are found. There is, indeed, 'nothing new under the sun.'

ELLICHPOOR, 1872.

CONTENTS.

THE BRIDE OF EMPIRE.

IN some wide waste of Toorkistan,
   Beside the Aral sea,
—Where little is seen of the works of man,
   And the desert stretches free,
For many a mile of marsh and fen,
   And many a league of sand,
And each black rock marks a tiger's den,
And high in air the vulture's ken
Is strained to catch the gleam of bones
That oft lie strewn among the stones
   In the track of some Tartar band,—
A wandering tribe their resting-place
Had made, and for a certain space

B

Sought in that pathless solitude

The simple means of living rude,

The desert draught, the hunter's food.

They were such as are born on a horse-hide, thrown

By the shady side of a giant stone;

As they are born, so are they nursed

In the gaunt embrace of Hunger and Thirst;

Their tender limbs are carried at speed

On the saddle-less back of the untamed steed;

Their rattle is the clanging quiver,

Their bath, the whirl of Jihoon's river;

Soft is their sleep on battle-field,

Rocked in the hollow of the shield.

Among these wanderers dwelt a man,

The rough mechanic of the clan,

Who mended bow and sharpened sword,

   And ground the arrow-heads of flint,

And cured the wounded of the horde

   With healing herbs, the desert lint;

Who erst, in queenly Samarcand,

 From Kazi wise or Moulla grave,

Had learned to form with skilful hand

 Those mystic signs, of power to save,

That long ago in Arab land

 The Prophet to the people gave.

For he could read the Kuran well,

And knew each wondrous miracle

Wrought by the Chosen of the Lord,

Or by the Master of the Sword;[1]

And those wild horsemen heard with awe

When he expounded Islam's law,

And called them, after battle done,

To praise the God through whom 'twas won.

The half of life o'er Kazim's head

 Had passed; he deemed it time to wed;

[1] Ali, the possessor of the sword Zoo'l-Fakan.

And after form of wooing brief,

He bought the daughter of a chief,

But not by dint of land or gold

—Things that the Tartars lightly hold ;—

And yet he gave a dowry rare,

To wit, five horses and a mare.

Pass we the bridal and the rest,

The least we say of these, the best.

But when the months their course had run,

In Kazim's tent was born a son

Whose lofty forehead token gave

That changeful Fortune was his slave,

And hope of highest destiny

Was dawning in his fearless eye.

His father saw, with joy and pride,

That much he bore and little cried,

Or if he wept, no single tear

Seemed starting from the fount of Fear,

But knitted brow and eye of fire

Gave warning of his infant ire.

His little fingers loved to feel
  The keen edge of the sword,
And he laughed at the glint of the glancing steel,
  When the warriors of the horde
Rode forth to fight with their weapons bright
  At the signal of their lord.

To him with growth it grew more dear
  To watch the arrows fly
To their goal in the heart of the dusky steer,[1]
  Or the eagle of the sky;
And he loved by the gleam of the glassy stream
  In the summer days to lie.

When the hunting falcon soared above,
  And the crocodile below
His long dark snout would swiftly move,
  His scaly head would show,
And a stain of blood, as he shot through the flood
  On the track of his speed would go.

[1] The Yak, or Ox of Thibet and Tartary.

He watched the forkèd lightning dart
  From the jet-black thunder-cloud ;
No touch of dread appalled his heart,
  Though the mountain oak was bowed ;
Though the waste around was filled with sound,
  And the storm-blast screamed aloud.

They called him Malik ; for the mystic signs
  That wise diviners read in face or brow,
The tender palm's pink interlacing lines,
  Conspired some lofty destiny to show ;
  And now the anxious father sought to sow
The seed of learning in the soil untilled
  Of his young heart ; that skill and force might
    grow
As twins together, and his mind be filled
With Power and Wisdom, strong to finish all he willed.

With curious hand and eager look
The stripling peeped within his book ;

He marked the ranked letters go
In ordered lines as warriors do ;
Or marshalled like a flight of cranes
That soar on high o'er Khata's[1] plains,
And in long column dense and black,
Veer never from their leader's track,
But stretch their tireless wings to gain
The fens that fringe the Aral main.

There Alif lifted high the spear,
And Ha the moony shield did bear,
    And Ba his bended bow ;
The crooked sabre Lam did wield
And Mim, conspicuous in the field,
    His helmet-crest did show. [2]

In vain the father strove to find
Some hidden nook in Malik's mind,

[1] Khata, called Cathay by old writers, is a name for Tartary.
[2] The forms of the letters are these :

ا   ه   ب   ل   م

Wherein the flaming love of strife
Not yet, perchance, had leapt to life :
And much he talked of hell and heaven,
Of penal fire, and sins forgiven ;
Of all the glories after death
Won by the worthies of the faith ;
Of the dark beam of Houri's eyes
Deep set in bowers of Paradise ;
Of the straight path that men must keep [1]
Or perish in the fiery deep ;
Of lesser and of greater sins,
And where right ends and wrong begins.
Still as he spoke, young Malik's eyes
Followed the wild swan through the skies ;
Or cast full many a longing glance
Where on the tent wall hung his lance ;
He seems his father's voice to hear,
But other sounds are in his ear ;

[1] The bridge to heaven, which passes over hell.

He lists to the tramp of the flying steed
Where horsemen hurl the ' light jereed ';
And he sighs, as comes from the mountain drear
The hungry tiger's voice of fear.

As time passed on, and lip and cheek
Of manhood's spring-tide 'gan to speak,
And the stiff muscle slanting stood
On his strong arm, as in mid flood
Of Jihoon stands some bar of stone,
And the swirling stream curls white thereon;
And his fair forehead, 'mid the clan
Of giants, taller by a span,
Shone o'er the lowering cloud of war
Like the silver round of the morning star—
Old Kazim, mindful of the words
That Muslims reverence like the Lord's,
That, ere his soul its prison broke,
The Comrade of the Prophet spoke;[1]

---

[1] Anas bin Malik, the last of the Companions of Mahommed.

' He of the faithful who hath wed,

One half his faith hath perfected,'—

One evening, in the twilight dim,

Called his dear son and spoke to him.

''Thy flower of youth is budding fair,

As the white lily in the stream,

That sucks the water and the air,

And turns to meet the morning beam ;

But sudden, from the mountain side,

In autumn sweeps the headlong tide,

A brown and boiling flood ;

Down falls the bank in dust and smoke,

Short from the stalk the flower is broke,

And down the foaming torrent whirled,

From side to side 'tis dashed and hurled

Mid rocks and trees and mud.

Alas ! fair blossom fresh and trim,

Thou bloomest aye on passion's brim :

Thy root is set in feeble clay

The Bride of Empire.

That soon in water melts away,

Thou needest, boy, a firmer stay.

'The silver moon is gilding now

The cypress on yon hillock's brow ;

Within that cypress sable shade

Gleams the white neck of a Tartar maid,

As, through the green sea of the south,

The pearl peeps from the oyster's mouth ;

Her father's bow[1] can call to war

The thousands of the wild Afshar,

Whose onset, like their arrows' flight,

Shoots on the foe too swift for sight ;

No need for me to tell her charms,

Well worthy of a warrior's arms,

To paint the depth of starry eyes

That move to shame the evening skies,

And all the wealth that nature showers

On face and form, in bounteous hours ;

[1] Equivalent to the Fiery Cross of the Highlands.

Thou knowest them well,

But only this to thee I tell,

That should'st thou choose the maid to woo,

She is thine own, her dowry too :

Her haughty sire my wealth doth know,

Won by the scymetar and bow,

And arts that gave my hand to hold

The charm that turneth steel to gold.'

Cold and unmoved the youth replied,

' Oh, father, I have sought a bride,

Since first I felt my pulses bound

At war-steed's snort, or trumpet sound,

A thousand times more fair than she

Or any maid of Tartary ;

Though small the wealth at my command,

Though nought is mine of house or land,

Yet far as spreads the desert sand,

And mountain chains, that herbless swell

From base as hot as nether hell

To crown of icy pinnacle ;

The portion that I woo withal
Is more than Khussan's treasures all.
My mistress never could be won
By all the mines unseen by sun,
That e'er have mocked the search of man
In farthest depths of Badakshan :[1]
Yet, father, is that treasure mine,
Whereby I'll win my bride divine,
And found, perchance, a royal line.'

Old Kazim shook his hoary head,
Gazed at his son, and doubting said,
' Where is this maid thou seekest then,
And where this dower unknown to men ?
What hoard is thine, I have not seen ?
Have Afreets, from the ocean green,
Slipped that lost gem thy finger on,
The potent seal of Solomon ?

[1] A country to the north of the Himalayas, celebrated for its rubies.

Or from the dark cave hast thou freed
The vanished cup of old Jamsheed?'

The son rose up from his father's side,
With stately step and glance of pride
   He passed into the tent ;
Returned anon, and in his hand
He bore a long and shining brand
   In graceful curving bent.
No jewel decked its iron hilt,
Its sheeny steel no gold had gilt,
But bright and keen the moonbeams played
Down the broad cold path of the stainless blade.

' The wife I woo,' young Malik said,
' Is fairer than a Tartar maid ;
   Circassia's curls I do not love,
   Nor Georgia's cheeks my heart can move :
   For the Bride of Empire waits for me,
   And the smiles of the Lady of Victory !

She is my life, my own adored,

And, lo ! her portion is the sword !'

Let the pearls have their birth

   In the depths of the sea ;

In the bowels of the earth

   Let the gold treasures be ;

It is not by these we can vanquish the Virgin of

   Sovereignty.

When the bowstring is strong,

   And the curve of the sword

Is sharp and is long,

   And the heart of its lord

Is bold, in the virtue of these things alone is the

   warrior's hoard !

When the lance is borne straight,

   And the arrow flies true,

And the battle-axe' weight
 Cleaves the helmet in two,
The maiden, Dominion, will listen to those who
 thus mightily woo.

So when few years had passed away,
In bleak Chorasmia Kazim lay,
 A wanderer at rest ;
But in the front of many a field,
His son that shining sword did wield,
 A conqueror confessed ;
Till high on Persia's ancient throne
He made that royal Bride his own
 To whom his troth he gave ;
And held her, till a mightier foe
In mortal conflict laid him low,
 The all-victorious Grave.

  Ellichpoor : *February*, 1872.

THE DEMON AND THE THIEF.

By Baghdád town a hermit dwelt
    Deep in the gloom of his ivied cave,
So very devout that he never went out,
    But pardon still for his sins did crave.

His beard on the floor, for a yard or more,
    Reposed, while he lifted his hands in prayer,
From his heels to his head, it could never be said,
    That he was in any part short of hair.

Like a dropping well, the walls of his cell
    Were crusted with fungi, and reeking with damp,
And often he'd sneeze, while he knelt on his knees,
    And his limbs and his joints were all twisted with
      cramp.

Thus wrapped in devotion, he'd never a notion
    Of asking for something to wrap himself in,
And heart, lungs, and liver did nothing but shiver,
    For no covering had they but his cuticle thin.

He'd many disciples, who thought him a saint,
    Then imagine their grief when they found him one
        day
Stretched out on the cold wet floor in a faint,
    For a beggar had taken his dinner away.

They remarked 'Inshah Allah,' expressive of pity,
    And wiped off the mud from his cheeks and his
        brow,
Then girding their loins they returned to the city,
    And brought him a fine young buffalo cow.

The holy hermit with many a prayer
    And blessing, their pious attention received,
And asserted that now he'd the milk of this cow,
    His petty privations were wholly relieved.

But a peasant, whose notions of 'meum and tuum'
 Were remarkably shady, did promise and vow
That by hook or by crook he would manage to do 'em,
 And quietly slope with that buffalo cow.

Not much did he care for curse or for prayer,
 Or the manifold books of the Doctors Four,[1]
But he made the remark, 'What a capital lark!'
 And started away for the hermit's door.

The sun went down, and the hill-tops brown
 Loomed hazy and dark through the twilight dim,
When he was aware of Somebody there
 Who seemed to be bent upon walking with him.

His hands, he observed, were remarkably curved,
 For each finger seemed tipped with a claw for a nail,
And he felt some fear, as he noticed in rear
 A something that looked very like a tail.

[1] The four doctors of Mussulman Law.

So after this cursory investigation
  Of his comrade's 'ensemble,' he felt rather blue,
But ventured to ask, not without trepidation,
  'Well, stranger, and pray who the devil are you?'

'You're very polite,' said that grim-looking wight,
  'But since I've a notion you're one of my flock,
For once I'll let out what I'm going about,
  As I do not suppose 't will your principles shock.

'Though they call me the devil, I always am civil
  To people who don't interfere with me;
I'm a foe to strife, and a quiet life
  With my own inclinations would truly agree.

'But the meekest doggie is sure to bite
  If you wantonly cabbage his poor little bone,
And I think I've a right to a wee bit of spite
  Against meddlers who *won't* let my business alone.

' There's a hermit here whom they call a Fakeer,
    Who really has given me cause for complaint ;
He does nothing but pray both night and day,
    And these ignorant asses all think him a saint.

' I should not object to his personal piety,
    For that is a part of his private affairs ;
But he's taken upon him to badger and fly at me,
    And abuse my pet traps and my favourite snares.

' Thus noon, night, and morning, he's always warning
    The people who flock to his wretched abode,
That the deeds of the Turks are a joke to my works,
    And that I am a snake, and a fox, and a toad.

' 'Tis true I might smile at comparisons vile,
    But somehow he seems to have found the way
To the heart of that zany, the monkey-like many,
    Who from pure imitation, have taken to pray.

' So absinthe and gin, and all sorts of sweet sin

    Are quite at a discount ; and rogues in a row

  In temp'rance processions make touching confessions,

    And the spout and the tea-pot incessantly flow.

' Good porter and swipes, and their long clay pipes

    By the " mobile vulgus " are wholly eschewed,

  This cranky old creature has done for the theatre,

    And even Aunt Sally, I'm told, is tabooed.

' As at each pious meeting he says life is fleeting,

    And that men should rejoice to be rid of their ills,

  I'll lend him a hand to the Promised Land

    With one of these very effectual pills.

' To night when his gruel he's eagerly brewing,

    And poking the sticks, with his back to the door,

  And his old shrivelled knees o'er the embers are stewing,

    As though he had ne'er seen a fire before,

' I'll quietly pop in, and speedily drop in
    The midst of the savoury steam and froth
This pill, which he'll take, and in half a shake
    'Twill help him, I trust, to his final broth.

' And now I've done speaking, you, sir, who are sneaking
    So gleefully up to the door of his cell,
I should like to hear too what you're going to do,
    So please have the kindness your story to tell.'

' There's a trifling present,' replied the peasant,
    ' In the shape of a buffalo, young and fat,
That a " son," as they term it, has given the hermit,
    A quadruped I am resolved to get at.

' He's so wrapped in religion, a cow from a pigeon
    He couldn't distinguish ; now isn't it waste
That on such an old muff a so beautiful buffalo
    Should be quite thrown away, when another *has*
        taste ?'

' Your reasoning really's most cogent,' said Satan,

 ' No caviller could find the least fault on that head,

And with logic thus true, you may well keep your hat on

 Before all philosophers, living or dead.'

Thus sweetly conversing, the hermit aspersing,

 To his lowly dwelling they soon drew near,

But the stream of discourse soon changed its course.

 As you, gentle reader, shall shortly hear.

Thus pondered the peasant, '"Twould hardly be pleasant,

 If a hue and a hubbub were raised too soon,

And the hermit in colic from draught diabolic

 Should bellow and howl to a very old tune ;

' For the folk would come running, and all my cunning

 Would never avail the cow to steal ;

Or suppose I were nailed by his friends, and impaled—

 I won't risk my bacon for beef, pork, or veal !'

' I'd this nice little scheme on,' reflected the demon,
  'When this blundering thief comes and puts in his oar;
For 'tis evident now that he can't steal the cow,
  Unless, in the first place, he opens the door;

'Now it's perfectly clear, should the hermit hear
  The door open, there'll be such a hullabaloo
That perforce I must beat a disgraceful retreat,
  A thing which I make it a rule not to do.

To the other said he, ' Now, look here, do you see,
  You must first let me do for the holy man,
Then off you can go with the fat buffalo;
  To manage them both 'tis the only plan.'

' No, no,' said the thief, ' I should come to grief
  If I worked in a fashion so very absurd;
You've only to wait till I'm clear of the gate,
  And I'll venture to say I shall not be heard.'

'Twas in vain that the devil held forth on the evil
　Of so palpably taking the cart for the horse ;
In ideas on the causative equally positive,
　The thief of *his* logic maintained the force.

Then in wrangling and fretting their interests forgetting,
　The flame of dissension broke out 'twixt the two,
And the fire of their anger grew stronger and stronger,
　And they cursed one another till all was blue.

' Hallo, holy hermit,' the peasant cried out,
　' This demon is seeking your reverence to slay ;'
' This beast of a peasant,' the demon 'gan shout,
　' Is intent upon driving your buff'lo away !'

The hermit arose from his couch of stone,
　And hearing the outcry, began to bawl,
Till the neighbours came tumbling in, everyone,
　This flourished a boot-jack, that brandished an awl.

Away went the devil, away ran the thief,

    Nor tarried a moment to make their adieus;

And they got such a fright on that terrible night,

    That never again did they plague the recluse.

And these words, there's no doubt, that good hermit

        did spout,

    Which now to a proverb of proverbs have grown;

Videlicet, 'Truly when rogues fall out,

    Honest folks generally come by their own!

THE KING AND THE FALCON.

FAIR of face and gallant of mien
The king rides forth to the forest green ;
The tawny hounds before him bay,
Behind him throng the huntsmen gay,
Around their lord the Oomara[1] press,
Each holds his hawk by the silver jess ;
Through thorny thickets horses dashing
Set every well-filled quiver clashing ;
'Tis merry the rattle of swords to hear
That thirst for the blood of the stricken deer,
To see the long glades of the forest old
Lit with the glimmer of steel and gold !
And the chirp of birds and the rustle of leaves
Are a certain salve for the soul that grieves,

[1] The nobles.

And the heart swells high with joyous pride,

And the knees are pressed to the horse's side :

And all that was left in the city behind,

And the manifold sorrows that clouded the mind

Have vanished away like a troublesome dream,

Or a swallow that glides o'er the breast of the
stream.

Proud of his jesses of golden twist

The falcon sits on the monarch's fist ;

Moved by nought, he keeps his place

With his keen dark eyes on his master's face ;

He waits in hope till the quarry shall rise,

And he be flung free to the field of the skies,

To stoop at his will from the height of the air,

And the eyes of the panting deer to tear ;

Or with wing too swift for huntsman's sight,

To follow the mountain partridge's flight

O'er sandy waste and hill-tops brown,

While horses stumble and riders are thrown.

But hark ! the tangled forest crashes,

As an antlered stag from the thicket dashes ;

Deep of chest, and speedy of limb,

With nostril broad and pastern slim,

Fleet is the hound that shall close with him !

Then many a hoof the dust did spurn,

As the blood leapt forth from the spur-stroke stern ;

Each fiery noble, quick as thought,

His ready bow from his shoulder caught,

Each runner swift his sandal shoe

In bush or gully heedless threw ;

And like leaves on the blast of the autumn wind

The hunt swept on that stag behind.

Many an arrow from many a bow

Whistles forth, as on they go :

But though dark with sweat is the quarry's hide,

No spot of blood has stained his side.

With head to northward pointed true,

He bursts the echoing woodland through :

The King and the Falcon.

The splintered branches round him fly,
Behind him swells the hunter's cry,
His tireless feet press on the more
To the boundless desert that lies before.

Now a glimpse of the waste he sees
Peep brownly through the emerald trees,
Now grassy glades are opening wide,
Now vanished is the greenwood's pride,
And now he's at the desert side.
Swifter still he holds his way
Toward the distant mountains grey,
Tower of strength to weary game,
Steep and craggy, crowned with flame.

Now many a panting steed was spent,
And many a chief his bow unbent;
The few staunch hounds the chase that ply,
Now, one by one, lie down and die :

A torrent's rocky bed and deep
Now yawns before, a desperate leap,
There is but one dare make the spring,
So all alone now rides the king.

Well had he need that his straining steed
Should come of Nejed's winged breed,
That swift as breath of Samoom fly
O'er central sands of Araby :
He was white as the snow-wreath bright
That shines from Alwand's topmost height,
From fetlock short to forehead broad
His skin no spot of colour showed,
Like a shooting star through a moonless night,
He followed the stag in his headlong flight.

Now high his hand the monarch threw,
Forth from his fist the falcon flew,
A moment paused in mid-career,
Then swooped on the astonished deer ;

No refuge he in speed could seek
From flapping wing and furious beak ;
A devious course in vain he tries,
The cruel talons find his eyes ;
Perforce he turns and stands at bay,
But sight and strength ebb fast away
He strives to shake his antlered crest,
But now the sword is in his breast ;
He staggers, falls ; one long-drawn groan,
His life is fled, the chase is done.

Down leapt the monarch to the earth,
Unloosed the curb, and slacked the girth,
Did off his cap with jewels set,
And wiped his brow with toildrops wet,
Sheathed his good sword, then gazed around,
To mark the spot and view the ground.
Just where the stag had fall'n in death,
A crag rose from the rugged heath,

D

Whose splintered top was all o'ergrown
With withered herbs and creepers brown;
Such plants as born in torrid clime
Give certain token of the time ;
In rain and flood they flourish green,
In burning sun are drooping seen,
 But never wholly die ;
And hang they brown or bloom they fair,
Who faints with thirst need not despair,
Where they can live, the wanderer there
 Will find some water nigh.

So now the king with heedful look
Explored that wild and silent nook ;
Burning his throat, and parched his lip,
He longed to hear the water drip :
And now behold where slowly ooze
Few drops, as bright as spring-tide dews,
Each liquid bead a fairer gem
To him, than diamonds on the hem

Of priceless robe that David's son
From vanquished Pari ever won.
A silver cup from his quiver he drew,
And held it under that dropping dew;
Impatiently he watched the brim
Of the water rise to the vessel's rim,
He was too hurried to taste or sip
But greedily lifted the cup to his lip.

Like lightning bolt, with sudden shock,
Down shot the falcon from the rock;
Dashed from his master's hand the cup—
Those precious drops the sand drank up.
The thirsty king, with angry look,
Again the silver goblet took,
Held it the scanty stream amid,
And oft the heedless falcon chid!
But soon his soul with pleasure thrilled—
The sparkling tide the vessel filled.

In haste he raised the liquid bliss,
The rim his lip did almost kiss,
When from the lofty crag amain
The watchful falcon swooped again !
The cup flew ringing on the ground,
The water flashed like fire around.
His thirsty longing unappeased,
The wrathful king the falcon seized,
In thoughtless rage, with frenzied stroke,
He dashed the bird against the rock.
With quivering claw he grasps the heath,
A moment sobs in pangs of death,
Turns on the king his glazing eyes,
And thus with glance reproachful dies.

But now the sound of flying feet
Heralds a running huntsman fleet ;
He loosed his leather mitharah full
Of pure spring-water fresh and cool,

The King and the Falcon.

Poured the bright stream in the silver cup,
On bended knee then raised it up.
' Not so,' his angry sovereign said,
' My draught's dear price I well have paid ;
See lying on the bloody clay
The bird who dared to disobey.
Look where these diamond drops fall slow,
Sign of some fountain's overflow,
Take thou the cup, ascend the hill,
And from the source the goblet fill.'
The huntsman, like a bounding stag,
Leapt swiftly up the towering crag ;
—Why does he blench, and backward start.
While creeps the life-blood to his heart ?

Like stinted gift from miser's hand,
The water trickled slow
From flinty rock to thirsty sand,
Then dripped the crag below ;

But lo ! where stretched in hideous death
A serpent lay that rock beneath ;
His gleaming coils and speckled crest
Upon the fountain's marge did rest,
    And ever and anon
The liquid venom would distil
From his huge jaws, and to the rill
    Would slide from stone to stone.
Thus limpid poison flowed beneath,
Whose every drop was certain death.

Back shrank the huntsman at the sight,
And darted downward from the height,
In haste his wondrous story told ;
Then sighed and wept the monarch bold,
In bootless grief his garments tore,
And writhed in pangs unfelt before,
Lifted the falcon from the earth,
And poured these words of sorrow forth :

' Anger has anguish for brother,

  Swiftly one follows another,

  But, ah me ! haste is their mother.

' Would that a king had the power

  To quicken the death-smitten flower,

  To turn back the march of the hour !

' Would that penance and fast

  Had virtue to bring back the past !

  But where patience fails, sorrow must last.

' Traitor to Love and to Faith,

  I have given my darling to death ;

  How canst thou tarry, oh breath !'

THE MOUSE AND THE FROG.

A MOUSE, 'tis said, an enemy to strife,
    Lived in a hole beneath a hollow tree,
He was unblessed with family and wife,
    From carking care he dwelt entirely free,
And his small voice in thanks he oft would raise,
And exercise his throat with hymns of praise.

Beside this tree there was a fountain clear,
    A gem of purest water, never seen
By eye of man ; so small, 'twas like a tear
    Wept by sad heaven on that desert green ;
But if its bounds were narrow, it was deep
And bright and sweet, unsoiled by ox or sheep.

And in that fountain dwelt a lonely frog,
  Who liked his own good company so well,
That he regarded kinsfolk as a clog,
  And lived a hermit in his watery cell:
And he would oft astound the morning breeze
By croaking forth batrachian harmonies.

One day he came as usual to the edge
  To see the world and take a little air,
And thrusting up his snout above the sedge,
  Joyous, determined all his joy should share,
And in such cadence wild his notes he rolls
As parts his hearers' bodies from their souls.

The mouse, who then within his dusky hole
  Was chanting hymns in treble small and sweet,
Forth to his mansion's entrance softly stole
  Intent to view the author of this treat,
But much confounded by that discord dread
Sat up and clapped his hands and shook his head.

The frog, when he this auditor beheld
   Making, he thought, those signals of applause,
With windy pride and flattered fancy swelled,
   And plied his bellows with distended jaws ;
And thought ' How pleasant such a friend as he !
A comrade dowered with love of melody ! '

'Twas all in vain that Prudence whispered low,
  ' With a strange species bind not friendship's chain ;
From good companions floods of pleasure flow,
   From evil, torrents of eternal pain ;
And since his kind is diverse from thine own,
Be thou as glass, and hold thou him as stone ! '

But heedless Vanity and Self-conceit
   Too strongly at his heart-strings 'gan to pull :
Said he, ' ' The interchange of thought is sweet,
   And solitude I find a little dull ;
'Tis time to let my cagéd heart go free,
And taste the joys of sweet society.'

Thus having pondered to the mouse he said,

   ' Dear sir, I see your mind and mine are one,

And since our spirits in such bonds are wed,

   Why should our bodies choose to live alone ?

Why should you heaven in dismal solo praise,

While I, below, my " De profundis " raise ?

 ' The thousand beauties of the earth and air,

   The limpid brightness of the water cool,

Are things at once so pleasant and so fair

   They lift my soul above this narrow pool :

And then for some dear comrade's voice I long

To join my own in sky-resounding song.

' Why will you shrink within the dungeon dark

   That you and yours delight to call a home,

When here no cruel man or beast doth mark,

   No ravening vulture ever dares to come ?

Then why the glorious sights of Nature shun,

The verdant meadow and the shining sun ? '

The listening mouse, who many a time had sighed
    To share his thoughts with some one true and kind,
In courteous tone with fitting words replied ;
    His smiling face displayed his willing mind ;
And then with most affectionate embrace
They sealed their friendship on that very place.

So often now upon the pebbly side
    Of that fresh fountain did their hearts combine
In the swift flow of conversation's tide,
    Or recitation of some thrilling line,
Or moved at once by inspiration strong
They strained their throats in their accustomed song.

One day the mouse to his companion said,
    ' It often happens, when I cannot sleep,
And some grief wakes again as from the dead,
    I long to call you from the water deep,
That so your words like balm may soothe my wound—
But then, ah me ! how seldom are you found !

' My puny voice can never reach your ear,

   When, seeking comfort in my woe, I call,

The air-waves vainly smite the fountain clear

   Which thus divides us like a crystal wall :

Oh, can we not some stratagem devise

Whereby, like wizard, I may bid you rise ? '

' Oh, dear companion ! ' cried the frog, much moved,

   ' What you complain of, I myself have felt,

And oft desired the presence that I loved,

   Condemned, alas ! in absence' fire to melt,

And chanced to your dark castle's gate to come

When adverse fate had sent you forth from home.

' And now what strange device can we employ

   That I from water may call you on land,

Or you, in pressing time of grief or joy,

   May summon me to meet you on the strand ?

If aught you've settled, speak in happy hour,

That dire Division so may lose his power.'

'Methinks,' the mouse replied, 'I've found a clue
    That, in the hand of Caution tightly held,
Will guide us easily this labyrinth through,
    As Ariadne Theseus did of eld ;
But you, beloved friend, a while give ear,
'Twas said, " 'Tis mine to speak and yours to hear."

' I will set off for the next market-town,
    And enter there some general chandler's shop,
And there will buy—but ah ! we've ne'er a "brown,"
    Or any article that I could " pop "—
Why then I'll steal—" convey " the wise it call—
Of the best twine or string a penny ball.

' This ball, unrolled, will stretch for many a yard,
    And will not break for hardest snatch or pull,
So that from motion not at all debarred
    We shall thereby attain our purpose full,
If each tie tightly one end to his leg ;
What telegraph so good as this, I beg ?

' Thus friendship's rivets will be firmly knit,
 And baffled Distance will be banished quite,
And free from dread of envious cut or split,
 The chain of Concord will our souls unite,
And while we conjugate *amat, amabit*,
Wondering, the world will say, " *Quis separabit ?*" '

The mouse's plan in practice straight they put,
 Hugging themselves on their ingenious scheme,
Whereby sweet Converse' door could ne'er be shut,
 Nor dam arise in Intercourse's stream,
And strict Connection, with such fastening true,
Would make their very bodies hardly two.

One day the mouse toward the fountain side
 Went forth, Association's string to pull,
But ah ! stern Sorrow comes in bitter tide
 Just when we deem the cup of gladness full !—
A sable crow swooped downward from the air,
And whiz ! high up the wretched mouse did bear.

The frog, reposing in the water deep,
    And venting croaks, expressive of content,
Was sinking gently into blissful sleep
    With many a fair illusive vision blent:
When lo! that string becoming quickly 'taut,'
Up in the air like flying fish he shot.

Tied by the leg, his poor head hanging down,
    The helpless frog was borne at speed along,
Till, when the crow had passed o'er dale and down,
    This wondrous sight attracted quite a throng,
Who staring open-mouthed, exclaimed 'Well, now!
To see a frog caught by a common crow!'

The frog, incensed, bawled out to those below,
  'Asses and idiots! use your eyes and see
I am not caught by this confounded crow,
    But bound in chain of strong calamity:
And now too late I learn the deep damnation
Of those not cautious in association!'

THE GREEDY CAT.

A Sultan's capital within
There dwelt a beldame poor and thin ;
Her skinny frame in rags was clad,
Her face with constant fasting sad,
Her bleared eyes dropped with rheumy tears,
A staff propped up her weight of years :
The filthy hole wherein she dwelt
Like nether Hades reeked and smelt,
A home of darkness to be felt :
A wretched hut, a narrow cave,
Like bigot's heart, or miser's grave,
Unfit for murderer, thief, or slave.

This dwelling, shunned by bat and rat,
Maintained a starved and meagre cat,

E

One of a faithful race, who still,

In wealth and want, in good and ill,

Affect the spot where first they're fed

With partridge plump, or coarsest bread.

But this poor cat, in happiest hour,

Had never even dreamed of flour,

In its imagination, meat

Was something not for cats to eat :

The passing scent of wary mouse

Through ruined walls of that dark house,

The print the foot of one had left,

By cat's eyes seen through Stygian cleft,

By it were held as daily food,

Its portion of the common good.

Or if, perchance, through happy fate

There strayed, where it in ambush sate,

Some mouse, some orphan unadvised,

How much that hapless prey it prized !

The fire of joy lit up its cheek,

'Twas carnival for full a week,

Its heartfelt thanks to Heaven it mewed,
And dallying much, the god-send chewed.

The diet of this ill-starred cat
Could hardly be a source of fat,
Hence it appeared on roof or tree a
Shadow, phantom, or idea.
No words our language doth possess
Could e'er describe its wretchedness.

One day, with languid nerveless paw,
And fainting heart and empty maw,
And many a slip and many a fall,
It climbed at last upon a wall ;
And looking round in wild despair,
And uttering piteous prayer and swear,
Upon a neighbouring roof beheld
A brother cat so puffed and swelled
With rolls of fat on form and face,
It hardly seemed of feline race ;

With looks of pride it gazed around
And uttered soft a purring sound,
With lazy tail it flicked the flies,
And licked its chaps and blinked its eyes.

When the starved cat this wonder viewed,
It lifted up its voice and mewed,
And then, inspired by fasting long,
Burst into voluntary song.

'Oh, whence art thou so plump and sleek?
And why am I so wan and weak?
Oh, happy brother, kindly speak
        And tell me !

' Why should'st thou lick thy greasy cheek,
While I must fast, and pine, and peak?
Oh, happy brother, kindly speak
        And tell me !

' Where dost thou go thy food to seek ?

Here hunger makes me yell and shriek ;

Oh, happy brother, kindly speak

   And tell me !

With stretch and yawn, the neighbour cat

Replied, ' I dine the Sultan's at ;

There, when the royal board they spread,

I snatch the meat, I steal the bread,

I lick the dishes, clean the plates,

Then here repose, and thank the Fates.'

' Sweet friend,' the beldame's cat exclaimed,

' What things are those that thou hast named ?

What taste has bread that great men eat ?

And oh ! what flavour has their meat ?

My richest food is broth or stews

That now and then my mistress brews,

Made of—alas ! I know not what—

They smack of cinders, tongs, and pot.

Few times a year a mouse I catch,
And glimpse of purest pleasure snatch.'

Yes,' said the other, 'in my sight
Thy form is like a spider's quite.
So little fat, such wealth of lean
Before on cat was never seen.
Thy meagre frame, thy skinny face,
Are perfect libels on our race.
Oh, could'st thou see the Sultan's board
And taste the things wherewith 'tis stored,
Thy bones, though dry as from the tomb,
In life renewed would haste to bloom.'

'Oh, brother!' venting sobs and sighs,
The fleshless cat entreating cries,
'Since thou hast found the golden key
That opens doors of luxury,
For pity's sake, and kinship old
Leave not thy fellow in the cold.

If thou to royal feast repair
Oh, let me too thy fortune share!
The charity thou shew'st to me
May ope the gate of heaven for thee.'

The spectre form, the piteous tale
Did on the neighbour cat prevail:
'Twas fixed that both, at evening fall,
Should boune them to the Sultan's hall.
But first the beldame's cat, in tone
Of rapture, made the compact known
To that old woman, lorn and lone;
For oft, we hear, in days of eld,
Such wondrous councils have been held.
Through spectacles with rims of horn
Gazing, she now began to warn,
And shook her head with aspect sage
And caution of experienced age.

'My dear companion,' thus she said,
'"Tis true with me thou'rt poorly fed,

Right few the scraps that I can spare,

Thy daily bread is simply air :

But if so few the means of life,

At least thou livest free from strife,

And if this house be close and dark,

For us 'tis safe as Noah's ark.

So mean a place no thief would mark ;

No tyrant to our humble home

In search of spoil or prey would come :

If sweet content the spirit bless,

What state so good as lowliness ?

But if thou go'st among the great,

Ah me ! I tremble for thy fate !

The soul that always seeks for more

In boundless wealth will still be poor,

The mind whose longings ne'er are stilled

With grave-dust only can be filled,

Sweet baits and viands fat beneath,

How oft is spread the snare of Death !'

The Greedy Cat.

With these wise saws that ancient dame
Fought long with Hunger's furious flame;
The more the flood of words she poured
The more the fire imperious roared,
And strong desire to dine and sup
Burnt faith and patience wholly up.
So when the hour appointed came
The cat's design remained the same.
Supported by its neighbour sleek
It turned its tottering steps and weak,
With many a stumble, many a fall,
To haven of the Sultan's hall.

But oh! to plague the hapless poor
What buffets Fortune has in store!
It chanced, the very day before
That stealing through ill-guarded door,
Of ravenous cats at least a score
With hideous yell and screech and roar

Had on the table rushed, and soiled
The cloth, and dragged the roast and boiled
With swearing much and caterwaul
All up and down the banquet hall :
In trying one bold thief to catch,
The Sultan's self received a scratch.
The royal wrath blazed up at this,
He swore each cat the dust should kiss,
And bade a band of archers wait,
Whose flying arrows, winged with fate,
Should swift convey to feline heart
Due retribution's dreadful smart.

All ignorant of ambushed bow
That cat, with stealthy pace and slow,
And sniffing nostrils forward thrust,
Approached at once the board august ;
Then maddened by the smell of meat
It rushed towards the royal seat,

But ere its teeth could touch the joint
It ate an arrow's piercing point!
All former thoughts of meat and bread
Its bleeding bosom instant fled,
But squealing worse than 'wry-necked fife'
It ran like fire to save its life.

'Alas, alas,' it panting said,
'Why did I leave our lowly shed,
    Our calm and quiet house?
Oh, might I reach that tranquil spot,
Henceforth 'twill be my only plot
    To catch the wily mouse!

'Oh, ancient Mistress, tried and true,
    How could I ever part from you
        In danger's path to roam?
No mention now of daintiest dish,
Of hash or stew, of game or fish,
    Shall tempt me forth from home!

' On greedy schemes imprudent bent

　I've learned the sweetness of content,

　And every erring cat can tell

　Le jeu ne vaut pas la chandelle !'

THE OLD WOMAN AND THE ANGEL OF DEATH.

Once an old woman, indigent and worn,
    Dwelt in an ancient house beside a waste,
Dead was her husband ; widowed and forlorn,
    Her hopes, she said, in heaven alone were placed.

But one tie bound her spirit to the earth,
    An orphan daughter, beautiful and young,
Her mother's sole companion from her birth,
    As fair a flower as ever poet sung.

But dire disease, it chanced, to that lone place
    Came with his blasting step and wasting hand,
He plucked the roses from the daughter's face,
    And made her pale and thin as willow wand.

Gone was the sprightly walk wherewith she left
 The house at morn to drive her mother's herd
To desert pasture ; of her voice bereft,
 No more she poured her notes like woodland bird.

Her stature, once as poplar straight and tall,
 A broken reed, on bed uneasy lay,
All day she wished that pleasant night would fall,
 Through dreary night she longed for opening day.

The aged mother, swallowed up in grief,
 Knowing no rest, with groans and tears prayed
That Heaven would spare this newly-budding leaf,
 This fresh green shoot, this young unspotted maid.

' Alas !' she cried, ' if Death is not content
 That both should live, lo ! *I* am ready, I !
My light of life is gone, my days are spent,
 'Tis time that I, poor useless wretch, should die !

' In life prolonged I have no hope of joy,

 But pain increases as the years increase,

Would I were where no sorrow can annoy,

 Lapt in the sweetness of eternal peace !

' So if my life a ransom can be made

 For her, more dear than thousand lives to me,

Gladly I'll pass through Death's most grateful shade

 To gain the light of immortality !'

One day while thus that ancient dame did grieve,

 And her sad heart for her sick daughter burned,

Before the accustomed time of falling eve,

 A straying cow from the wild waste returned.

Into the kitchen walked the errant cow,

 Thirsty, regardless of domestic rule,

And in a vessel plunged her nose and brow,

 Full of good broth, in corner placed to cool.

When not a single drop of broth remained,
    The cow made efforts to withdraw her nose,
But all in vain; it stuck as though 'twere chained;
    So pot and all, away in fright she goes.

Hither and thither through the house and yard
    The maddened cow with many a bellow ran,
And knocked her head 'gainst wall and doorway hard,
    And made a fearful clattering with the pan.

The mistress rose in haste from bended knees,
    And went to learn what this dread noise might be;
Oh, how her heart stood still and blood did freeze
    When that strange raging monster she did see!

She thought this Being sure was Izráil,
    Death's awful angel, come at last to slay,
And instant terror 'gan her bosom thrill
    Lest he had come to take *her* soul away,

Her many tears and prayers she clean forgot,
  Her wish to be her daughter's sacrifice ;
In fear and horror rooted to the spot,
  For the bare life she screamed to pitying skies.

She cried with trembling limbs and streaming eyes,
  'Oh, mighty angel, *I* am not the one !
'See, see ! in yonder chamber sick she lies,
  Take *her* away, she is indeed thine own !

' I am her mother, I have no disease,
  But ah ! I have not very long to live ;
Then take my daughter, who is ready, please,
  And me till fated day short respite give !'

F

THE GARDENER AND THE BEAR.

'Tis merry, I ween, in a garden green
   To walk amid bushes and flowers and fruit,
      Where the damascene
      And the kidney bean,
   And everything else, doth flourish and shoot:

Where the rosy-cheeked apple burns rosy and red
   As a farmer's face through a quickset hedge,
      And the peach on the wall,
      And the raspberry small,
   Like whetstones sharpen the appetite's edge:

And the bright yellow ball of the orange is framed
   In the background dark of the changeless yew,

And the lily white
Springs fresh and bright
By the side of nemophila, lovely and blue.

And the nightingale calls to the bursting rose,
Or the blackbird sings from the hawthorn tree—
Both in West and East,
So I've heard at least,
Such a pearl of a garden you'll frequently see.

And 'tis said that in such a fair garden as this,
There dwelt an old peasant, ungainly and rough,
Who all his days
Had done nothing but raise
Cauliflowers, onions, and artichokes tough.

His affections were set upon early peas,
And asparagus' charms his heart beguiled,
A new apple-graft
Sent him perfectly daft,
And a seedling's decease made him cry like a child.

The red beet-root and white celery shoot
  Were fairer to him than a maiden's face,
      He would kneel in the mud
      Whole days, and bud
  On the briar-stocks scattered all over the place.

And oft he would sit on a wall or a gate
  Where that beautiful garden he best could view,
      And chuckle for hours
      O'er his fruits and his flowers,
  Each graceful shape and each brilliant hue.

And had he been any way given to verse
  There's not the least doubt he'd have chanted the
        praise.
      Of each blossom and plant he
      Had tended, as Dante
  And Petrarch their strains to their ladies would
        raise.

His heart, like a Dryad's, was bound up in trees,

    To the animal kingdom he'd little to say,

        He never could 'freeze'[1]

        To his own species,

    And few were the persons who came that way.

He had no desire for a son or a daughter,

    For he was too fond of himself to wish

        To gather a fig

        Or a 'tater' dig,

    Except just to furnish his own little dish.

But at last it so happened he managed to catch

    That cramp of retirement, a fit of the blues,

        And Solitude's smart

        Affected his heart

    And got through the rind of his feelings obtuse.

---

[1] American for 'take a liking.'

He'd no one to whom he could utter his woes,

Or the overstrung bow of his spirit unbend,

And his mind to disclose,

To the violet or rose

He found worth but little—without a friend !

The spectre of loneliness haunted his steps

In shady alley or sunshiny lawn,

He had no delight

In the balmy night

And he dreaded the flush of the breezy dawn.

So one day in despair, tired of wandering there,

He turned his sad face to the distant hill,

That perchance he might find

Some relief for his mind

In the desert that no one would sow or till.

He walked o'er the breadth of the dreary plain
  To the skirt of the mountain, rocky and grey,
    And the troublesome chain
    Of his lonely pain
  Was broken in two in a very odd way.

For it chanced that a Bear who lived up there,
  And was used in the caves and the hills to roam,
    Without any he
    Or affectionate she
  To make matters easy and pleasant at home:—

It chanced that this bear, to take the air,
  Had started off, weary of dwelling alone,
    And eager to meet
    With some comrade sweet
  To the bush-covered base of the mountain had gone.

The Bear was growling in sorrowful style
  When he stopped in surprise at a curious sight—
    That Gardener old,
    Who was pacing the wold,
  And banning the Powers of darkness and light.

The Bear saw the Gardener, the Gardener the Bear,
  Each felt Fate had sent him the wished-for friend,
    And they interchanged vows
    With hugs and bows,
  And their way to the garden did joyfully wend.

And whatever was meet of those fruits so sweet
  To his follower strange the Gardener gave,
    And the man and the brute
    So exactly did suit,
  That the Bear came and went like a dog or a
    slave.

When the master slept, the attendant kept
  A careful watch by his honoured bed,
    And with angry paw
    Would endeavour to claw
  The flies who *would* buzz round his face and his
    head.

One day when the Gardener according to wont
  Was sleeping at noon in the shade of a tree,
    A number of flies
    On his forehead and eyes
  Came settling and rolling in midsummer glee.

'Twas in vain that his paw in a constant see-saw
  The Bear kept shaking on this side and that ;
    When he saw that the flies
    His attempts did despise,
  He said, ' I'll come down on them heavy, that's flat !'

Then uplifting a stone of at least half-a-ton,

 He pounded it down with a terrible crash,

  And, as you may suppose,

  The poor Gardener's nose

 And his eyes, mouth, and brains, were reduced to a

  mash.

And hence they have said that a wise enemy

 Is better by far than an ignorant friend;

  And that if a man passes

  His time among asses,

 He's certain to get a good kick in the end !

THE DEVOTEE AND THE JAR
OF HONEY.

' ONCE on a time' in some Eastern clime,
 There lived a Devotee
Who cared for nought save heavenly thought
 And the hopes of eternity.

He seldom slept, but often wept
 And passed the day in prayer,
And at eve would stray along the way
 To breathe the cooler air.

Hard by a Merchant dwelt, possessed
 Of hives and linden trees,
From which would come the constant hum
 Of never-tiring bees.

The Merchant marked that holy man
How sad his face and brow,
Like a yew that waves o'er many graves
When the winds of winter blow.

He heard how poor he was and lone,
How pure and kind his soul,
How in hunger and thirst he still prayed on,
Nor borrowed, begged, or stole.

'I have meat and bread,' the Merchant said,
'And honey and oil also,
Sure some I can spare for my brother there
Who liveth in want and woe !

'For strength and health, and lands and wealth,
To men, I ween, were given
That their souls they might lift by dole and gift
To the treasure-house of heaven.'

So day by day the Merchant sent
  From his abundant store
A portion meet of his honey sweet
  To be left at the poor man's door.

The holy man with thanks and prayers
  And tears the present took,
A little he ate and the rest he set
  Aside in a secret nook.

In that secret nook an earthen jar
  High on a shelf he placed,
And his daily store in it would pour,
  And never a drop would waste.

Bright dreams of wealth and thoughts of pelf
  In his mind began to rise,
And oft he would think of the jar on the shelf
  When his heart should have been in the skies.

In that jar to peep was food and sleep
 And balm for sorrow and sin ;
And himself he would pinch to add an inch
 To the golden flood within.

Beneath the shelf he sat one day
 In that quiet corner cool,
He felt too gay to go and pray
 For the jar was almost full.

He said to himself, ' The times of woe
 For me are nearly past,
Though the wind of trouble strongly blow,
 Thank God, it lulls at last.

' And now 'twere well my store to sell,
 Good honey's a precious thing ;
Now, let me see—It well may be
 That dirams[1] ten 'twill bring.

---

[1] A diram is worth about twopence sterling.

'Ten dirams is a goodly sum ;
    I trow I shall not lose,
  If with them I from a shepherd buy
    Five young and likely ewes.

'For twice a year those ewes will bear
    Two healthy lambs apiece—
  There'll be twenty head ere a year be sped
    And many a goodly fleece.

' 'Tis well, 'tis well—and how to tell
    Their number in *ten* years?
  So vast a flock doth my reckoning mock— .
    What work for knife and shears !

'Search through the land on every hand,
    Whose substance will match mine?
  I will court some dame of noble name,
    Perhaps of royal line.

' A palace high and wide I'll build
　　To bring my bride unto,
　The spacious floor with gold I'll gild,
　　And the ceiling shall be blue.

' With many a coloured lamp the walls
　　At night shall shine like day,
　And fountains fresh and waterfalls
　　Shall dash their sparkling spray.

' And when the long-expected hour
　　And wished-for moment come,
　A darling son, a princely flower
　　In beauty there shall bloom.

' No bud beside the Ganges wide
　　Shall blush so fair as he ;
　His face shall be bright as the foam-flake white
　　Where the river meets the sea.

' And when his years of life attain
  The lucky time of four,[1]
I will instil in heart and brain
  The rudiments of lore.

' From height to height of learning's hill
  His little feet shall rise ;
With various tongues his mind I'll fill
  And deep philosophies.

' And should the headlong tide of youth
  In disobedience swell,
I'll bid him turn towards the truth
  And shun the pains of hell.

' And should my teaching not prevail
  His erring soul upon,
With this stout staff I will assail
  The tempting Evil One ! '

---

[1] The age at which Mussulman children commence their studies.

G

The holy man, thus wrapped in thought,
   Raised up his staff to smite,
Alas ! the blow to ruin brought
   That jar of honey quite !

Down through the board like rain it poured
   O'er hair and face and beard,
No insect drunk in treacle sunk,
   Was ever so besmeared !

Bitter his tears, for schemes of years
   At once dissolved away ;
But soon he rose, and washed his clothes ;
   Resolved to fast and pray.

AN EPISODE OF SA'DI.[1]

TRIPOLI town is a lovely sight,

'Twixt the merry blue sea and the mountain white :

The mountain of ten thousand snows ;

The sea, alive with thousand prows ;

The battled walls, whose highest tower

Is bright with sunset's crimson shower,

The Red Cross, waving fair and free,

Far seen by land and eke by sea;

The pluméd helms of the warriors tall ;

The lance-heads glittering on the wall ;

The purple grapes, in vineyards low

Beneath yon hillock's rocky brow ;

[1] Born A.D. 1176.

The varying crowds that ceaseless pass
To market, musjid, or to mass :—
Such sight is fair to all men, save
To two, the captive and the slave !

Below the wall, behold the trench
Where labouring hundreds toil to wrench
The earth-fast rock from the stubborn waste,
While whip and rod compel their haste;
   A motley crew are they.
There the lithe Arab, foe to work,
Digs by the side of stalwart Turk,
And the fair Koord, with eyes of blue,
Pulls at one rope with the swarthy Jew :
Unwillingly their limbs they move,
But the stern Norman stands above,
   And they perforce obey.
Though each of them to other bears
The hate that springs from many years

Of mutual wrong and strife and crime
That fill the page of Eastern time,
Yet here united, all detest
Their mail-clad masters from the West.
As well may black combine with white,
As soon may day be mixed with night,
As East and West in love unite.
The soldiers strive, with warnings loud,
To urge to work the weary crowd;
The while each slave, in language terse,
Utters his nation's deepest curse.
But see, apart there standeth one
Whose daily task is 'smoothly done,'—
Whose heart nor lips are prone to curse,
Who murmurs now an ancient verse
In the soft tongue that Sheeráz maids
Speak softly in Musalla's shades;
'Sorrow is good for patience's sake,
  Through darkest night the dawn will break.'

And now his thoughts have wandered far
   Towards the morning land
Where rises mighty Istakhar,
And Jamshced's throne, that Peace and War
And Time and Change have failed to mar :
   And now he sees the strand
Of that fair gulf that Paris[1] love,
Through whose green depths the coral grove
And pearly shells are seen——
' Sa'di ! this face is surely thine !'
Has brought him back to Palestine.

Before him stands, in flowing gown,
An ancient friend from Halab's[1] town,
And joy and pity and surprise
Are mingled in his face and eyes.
' Thou amongst slaves ! all mire and sand,
In chains ! a pickaxe in thy hand !
How cam'st thou here from Irán land ?'

[1] Fairies.   [2] Aleppo.

' Oh, friend,' the poet smiling said,

In fair Damishk,[1] I lately stayed,

But Nature me a wanderer made.

I cannot brook, for many days,

To see the light of morning rays

Gild the same waters, trees, or ways.

E'en in Damishk, though sweet at first,

I thought my prisoned heart would burst.

I longed to leave the throngs of men,

And dwell in desert lone again ;

To feel once more the morning air

Breathe on my brow, unvexed by care,

And at still eve, to pour my prayer,

Myself sole priest and worshipper.

So leaving mosque and minaret,

My face toward the West I set,

And roamed the sacred wilderness

Where Those have trod whom all men bless,

---

[1] Damascus.

And Christian, Jew, and Muslim meet
To kiss the print of holy feet.
Glad was my heart what time I heard,
Through mountain wood, each tuneful bird
In many a varied strain of praise
Lauding our God, His works and ways:
Sweet 'twas to hear through rustling trees
The soft response of whispering breeze;
Or standing on the lonely shore
To catch, through furious dash and roar,
The anthem of the stormy seas.
I saw, upon the hoary brow
Of Lebanon, the cedars bow,
The willows bent o'er Jordan's flood,
The fir trees stooped in Carmel's wood :
Each tree and rock, each flower and sod,
Seemed only made to worship God !
Rapt from the world, I heedless went,
And wandered near the Frankish tent ;

And now, a slave, I labour here—
What matter? Heaven is always near!'

'Not so, my friend,' the other said,
'Thy ransom shall be straightway paid,
And soon for joy exchanging woe,
With me to Halab shalt thou go.'
The merchant (such his trade) was known
To Christian leaders in the town;
Money has power in peace and wars,
For ransom small of ten dinars,[1]
He freed the sweetest bard of Fars.

That merchant had a daughter fair,
In curtained Haram nursed with care:
One of those flowers whose lovely sheen
Is doomed by man to 'blush unseen,'

---

[1] A dinar was worth about thirty pence.

And be she maiden, be she wife,

Sees but the prison side of life—

   But Woman still is she,

And so her lord will often find

That though he fetter mould and mind,

   Her tongue is always free.

The merchant now this daughter gave

To Sa'di, late the Christian's slave,

With hundred gold dinars for dower,

And all that decks a bridal bower.

Alas ! delight can never last,

After joy's feast oft comes a fast,

   And so the poet found ;

His dark-eyed spouse right soon began

   To pass the common bound

That marks the plain of friendly strife

'Twixt loving husband, duteous wife:

   Her woman's pride arose,

Little recked she of verse or prose,

And measured Misia', balanced Beit, [1]
Were all in vein to check her spite ;
She lacked the power in him to find
That genius bright, that master mind
That could the whole wide East beguile
From China's wall to source of Nile.
The great are seldom great at home,
   Their powers, that sun-like stream
Without, are dim when there they come,
   A rushlight's flickering beam ;
The eloquence, whose wondrous power
   Can sway a lawless throng,
Has little might in quiet hour
   Against a woman's tongue.
Do what he would, he could not please,
When he was summer, she would freeze,
When he would sleep, why she would wake,
And every hour some whim would take.

   [1] Misia', a hemistich. Beit, a couplet.

At last she cried, 'That I should have

A husband who was once a slave!

How oft I would dream of some dauntless Ameer

   Some gallant and handsome lord,

Who had ridden a tilt with a Norman spear

   And dared the Frankish sword!

Some valiant noble who would come

   Borne on his piebald steed,

Like Moo'tasim,[1] from his distant home,

   To succour his lady in need!

And after those sweet dreams I see

A husband brought me such as *thee!*

Pray art not thou the captive found

By my fond sire on Christian ground,

A wretched serf, who toiled all day

At lifting stones and digging clay?

And such as *thou* must I obey?

---

[1] Referring to the Arabic account of the taking of Amoria, when everyone was said to have been mounted on a piebald horse.

Did he not give to set thee free,

Twice five dinars, too much for thee?'

' ''Tis true,' the poet sadly said,

Though well, I trow, that sum I've paid;

E'en so the shepherd saves the sheep

From wolves that near the sheepfold creep,

And after gives the ransomed life

A prey to cruel butcher's knife !

For ten dinars he set me free

   From Christian bonds, my wife;

But for one hundred tethered me

   To thee, a slave for life !'

HAJAJ[1] *AND HIS CHAMBERLAIN.*

CRUEL Hajaj, as the chroniclers say,
　Though he'd little respect for a hand or a head,
Though noses and fingers he lopped away
　As a gardener does an asparagus bed ;

Possessed notwithstanding a great partiality
　For a certain old chamberlain, largely endued
With one speciality—knowing the quality
　Of all the good liquor that ever was brewed.

So oft 'on the quiet,' when firman and fiat
　Were written and issued, and business was done,
And cutting and flaying, and slicing and slaying,
　Had each had their turn till the set of the sun ;

[2] A cruel Governor of Irak, under the Omiad Khalifs.

In his private divan, with this jocund old man,
    He would sit and hobnob, and each deep stern line
On his pitiless brow would softer grow
    O'er a brimming flagon of Sheeráz wine.

They drank and they gossipped of matters and things,
    And the various troubles that harass our lives,
Till they got to one, common to beggars and kings,
    To wit, the unspeakable bother of wives.

Said Hajaj, ' They are brimfull of fancies and wiles,
    And no one can tell what they next will be at— .
Such a marvellous compound of whimper and smiles—
    Trust my wife ! Why, I'd far rather trust a cat !'

Said the chamberlain, ''Tis so with many, my lord,
    Nay, 'tis so with most ; but I wish that my life
May be suddenly brought to an end with the sword
    If I do not believe in my own dear wife !

' She's lovely and sweet, and so very discreet
    That stories and scandal she soons cut short;
And for days together she'll talk of the weather,
    And never ask once about news from the court.

' If I come home late, she'll not question or prate,
    Nor angrily ask, "Where on earth have you been?"
But simply say, " Have you had a nice day?"
    And then she will hand me paijamahs[1] clean.

' If I tell her some matter, no fear of *her* chatter;
    From her faithful soul no vent 'twill find,
She's so perfectly safe, on the summit of Kaf[2]
    She'd not even whisper a word to the wind !'

Said Hajaj, ' Oh, my friend, let us hope your end
    May never depend on womankind,
For I can of all you say point out the fallacy
    In a way that for ever will change your mind.

       [1] Loose drawers.   [2] Caucasus.

' Now take this bag with the sacred seal

    Of the Khalif (God shield him) impressed thereon ;

You must tell your wife that you happened to steal

    (Heaven willed it) this gold, which belongs to the

        throne.

' With many a kiss and with many a prayer

    You must beg her to keep this secret well,

For that if the affair should chance to take air,

    Why—your head to the dogs and your soul to hell.'

The chamberlain promised his lord to obey :

    Of his lady's discretion no doubts had he,

And gaily he carried the cash away

    To the house where he lived with that excellent she.

With many a kiss and with many a prayer

    He showed the bag and his story told :

And sweet 'twas to see the delight of the fair,

    As she fondled her husband and collared the gold.

'You sharp little rogue,' she endearingly said,

   'Oh, *how* did you manage Hajaj to do?

And what secret of yours have I *ever* betrayed?

   Do you think I've turned parrot, you sceptical Jew?'

Now when many a day had passed away,

   The wily Hajaj to his chamberlain gave,

With aspect pleasant, a nice little present,

   In the shape of a pretty young Georgian slave.

But alas! such a smile, such a look full of guile

   Had the Lady of Discord, when Pallas and Herè

For the sake of her apple began to grapple

   And spoiled all the fun of the festival cheery.

With sobs and with sighs and with tears in her eyes,

   The news of this present the dame received,

And exclaimed 'Did you ever?' and then 'No I never!

   Such wickedness really who could have believed?'

Her husband not yet did she openly scold,

    But her answers grew short and her face grew long.

And for days together the dinner was cold,

    So at last he perceived there was something wrong.

' My dear,' said he, ' I can plainly see

    That something or other has put you out ;

If so, now pray why can't you say

    At once what's the matter, not sulk and pout ? '

' I would rather be fried,' all in tears she replied,

    ' Than utter a word or a syllable say ! '

Then her protest ignoring, in accents imploring,

    Cried ' *Do* send that odious creature away ! '

' My love,' said the chamberlain, 'what can I do ?

    She's the governor's gift, and I do not choose

His favours to slight, when he's been so polite,

    And besides—I have only got one head to lose.

Not at all like a tonic, this answer laconic
   Stirred the lady's bile to a frightful degree;
Not a word she said, but nodded her head,
   And under her breath muttered ' We shall see !'

That bag she took from its dark snug nook,
   That bag with the Khalif's seal impressed,
And when day was spent, away she went
   With the cash hidden carefully under her vest.

She walked up straight to the palace gate,
   And gave the door such a thundering knock,
That the porter snoring, all things ignoring,
   Fell clean off his bench with the fright and the
     shock.

Himself then shaking, his bunch of keys taking,
   He opened the door with astonishing speed,
For he thought that the dead must be certainly waking,
   Or that Iblis from limbo was suddenly freed.

To his great surprise, in female guise,
 A person he saw, who thus began,
' Come, time don't lose, I've particular news,
 So let me in to your master, young man !'

The porter required but little persuasion,
 For scandal whispered 'twas not very rare
For Hajaj to receive, as on this occasion,
 A private visit from some of the fair.

When the chamberlain's wife in the presence august
 Arrived, she performed the obeisance due ;
' Your highness,' she said, 'will forgive me, I trust ;
 My motive to this was devotion to you :

' My husband, my lord, (may his features be blackened !)
 Has been your chamberlain many a year,
And the bonds of fidelity how has he slackened !
 Alas ! to inform you I almost fear ;

' I've the strongest objection to tales and to slander,
　　And he is my husband, a brute though he be ;
But my duty to you and the sacred Commander
　　Of the Faithful, shall ever be first with me !

' The truth must be told that this bag of gold,
　　Impressed with the holy Khalif's seal,
He brought away from the palace one day,
　　And said "'twas a trifle he'd managed to steal."

' This secret long on the tip of my tongue
　　I have carried, a martyr to duty and love ;
"Have a care," one said, "for your husband's head !"
　　Cried the other, "A dutiful subject prove !"

' So I leave him now to your highness' mercy
　　And justice, which every day active we see,
For since he's made free with the public purse, he
　　Is certainly not fit to live with me.'

Said Hajaj, 'Ma'am, your visit's not quite unexpected,
  Nor your kind information entirely new ;
'Tis all the result of a plan I projected
    To teach your poor husband the truth about you.'

Then he bid them summon the chamberlain straight,
  Who hastened in, much surprised to see
His dumb-foundered spouse in a fainting state,
    And Hajaj with the bag of gold safe on his knee.

' My friend,' said the Governor, ' be pleased to perceive
    The trick your wise excellent wife has played ;
And no woman, perhaps you will now believe,
    Is worthy of trust, be she matron or maid :

' For had not this play been arranged one day
    For a certain purpose, betwixt you and me,
The boys would be bowling, the dogs would be rolling
    Your head down the gutter, with frolic and glee !'

THE HYPOCRITICAL CAT.

Within the border of a mountain high
　　A speckled Partridge once his nest had made,
And took delight alone to walk and fly
　　And plume his feathers in the pleasant shade,
And unobserved with sprightly steps would move,
And send his merry cry through all the grove.

But Time, that alters so the minds of men,
　　O'er bird and beast, no less, doth ever reign :
All love to change the mountain for the glen,
　　Anon, to pass to hill-top from the plain ;
There is no creature of the earth or sea
That's not enamoured of sweet Liberty.

And so that Partridge, tired of always seeing

    The same grey landscape through the same green

        grass,

And feeling Freedom's impulse stir his being,

    Resolved some time in other lands to pass,

And, after having thus refreshed his mind,

Returning home, his desert nest to find.

But after he'd been gone a little while,

    A Quail, who lived not very far from thence,

Thinking that nest of a superior style,

    Resolved to profit at its lord's expense,

And straightway took up his abode therein,

Saying ' To leave it empty were a sin.'

But lo ! to his surprise and great chagrin,

    After some months the Partridge reappeared,

And much in wrath, cried ' Sir, pray what d' you mean ?

    Have you the impudence to come and beard

Me in my very nest? Come, mizzle, fly !

Or you and I shall quarrel speedily.'

' Quarrel or not,' the angry Quail replied,

  ' I'm in possession, and I shall not move,

One day I found this nest unoccupied,

  So that it's yours I don't see how you'll prove ;

Your threats and struts I value not a pin,

Do what you like : you're out and I am in.'

So after some time they had vainly passed

  In question wrathful and quick repartee,

Becoming tired, it was agreed at last

  That they should put the case in equity,

And seek some learned judge, who would decide

Which of the claimants Right had justified.

The Partridge said, ' Hard by there dwells a Cat

  Who earthly cares and worldly love has left,

Who injures neither bird nor mouse nor rat,

  Whose heart of evil passions is bereft,

Who seeks continually the way of heaven

And aye with holy texts his speech doth leaven.

'And from the time when in the morning sky
      The sun's red rim above the waste is seen,
To that sweet hour when from the plain on high
      The stars, embattled, shine in splendour keen,
The portal of his mouth no food doth pass—
And all he breaks his fast on is dry grass.

' But not content with this, when night comes on
      And the last flush has vanished from the West,
He utters prayers with many a tear and groan,
      Nor bathes his eyelids in the balm of rest ;
And till again the white dawn climbs the East
His soul from wrestling never is released.

' 'Tis best that we should now refer to him,
      Nor waste our time in profitless debate ;
He will pour wisdom on our vision dim,
      And our dark thoughts with light illuminate,
And far from dallying with our trust and awe,
Will bare the *penetralia* of the law.'

The Quail consented, and away they went
    To seek the cell of that serene recluse,
Who, when he saw them coming, straightway bent
    His knees, whose fur was worn by constant use,
And turned his countenance towards the shrine,
And breathed a prayer with many a pious sign.

The prayer was lengthy, and aloof they stood
    Until his worship should have finished quite,
Besides, the warning current of their blood
    A little paused at that peculiar sight,
And while his piety they marvelled at
They could not quite forget he was a Cat.

At last, with many a sigh and upward look
    Until his pupils were completely hid,
His bowed head several times he gently shook ;
    And then those two in small soft whisper bid
To state their business, and to please be quick,
For he with heavenly desire was sick.

Then each his case with artless eloquence
    Began to urge ; but the judge seemed to catch
But here and there the thread of evidence,
    And now and then his ears and nose did scratch ;
And said anon, ' Young friends, be pleased to bear
With my infirmities ; I cannot hear.

' Alas ! my youth was spent in Folly's maze,
    Unguided by the clue that leadeth well ;
I passed the reckless spring-tide of my days
    In search of things that please the taste and smell ;
And now my senses fade in wintry blast
Of weak old age : what mortal power can last ?

And since my senses then offenders were,
    'Tis meet and right they should be punished now,
Although in bitter penitence of prayer
    From night till morn my weary knees I bow ;
But small, I know, the use of agèd breath,
And limbs that totter on the verge of death.

'But if you fancy that experience sad
    Reaped in my mis-spent life, at all avail
To make you separate good things from bad,
    And valid Justice from Self-interest frail,
I would entreat you to draw somewhat near,
That so the *pros* and *cons* I well may hear.

'And kindly speak a little louder too,
    That I no tittle of the case may lose,
And may adjudicate with conscience true
    And neither me of favour may accuse ;
But ere, O litigants, you plead your cause,
Beware you trifle not with heavenly laws.

The petty quibbles of an earthly court,
    A word erased, or an undotted i,
A measure by a hair-breadth long or short,
    Illegal action, doubtful alibi,
All these count nothing in the court of heaven,
Where by Truth only is the judgment given.

' Therefore bethink you of the real state

 Of the affair, and search your conscience well,

And if in aught that mentor hesitate,

 Beware how that is evidence you tell ;

For what avails it gold or lands to gain ?

They all must perish, but our souls remain.

' And this is all that I demand as fee,

 That you should listen to my counsels grave,

And in all things should act with equity,

 And learn, to give is better than to have,

And free your spirits from the load of Self,

And filthy trammels of the love of pelf.

' And know, oh plaintiff and defendant both,

 That whoso has the right upon his side,

Though he gain not his suit, yet vanquish doth,

 And in the angels' eyes is justified ;

But he who by unlawful means doth win,

In hottest flame must expiate his sin.'

Thus with sta'e truth and ancient platitude

   He poured his poison in their silly hearts,

And by degrees their minds with trust imbued,

   And dull oblivion of his cat-like arts;

And so they 'gan a little nearer draw

Till he could almost reach them with his paw.

' And now,' quoth he ' young friends, let us unite

   In one short prayer before our work begins,

That heaven may guide us in our task aright,

   Or if we err, may pardon all our sins ;

And when I utter the Great Being's name,

Bow down your heads, and worship at the same.'

Then he, with whiskered visage bland and meek,

   Began to drawl in softly-lisping tone

A supplication from the poor and weak

   Against the proud and strong ; and soon his drone

Produced so great a stupor in their brains

That Slumber all but bound them in his chains.

But at the name divine, with sudden jerk,

    They bent their heads together to the ground ;

Whereat that ever-fasting pious Turk

    Darted upon them with a furious bound,

And showing vast activity of jaw,

Conveyed their flesh to his abstemious maw.

And hence the sages of the East have said,

    All things to their own nature will return ;

The nourishment of men dwells aye in bread ;

    Water will drown, and fire will always burn ;

Trust not what seems unusual and strange,

For outward semblance shows not inward change.

THE GEESE AND THE TORTOISE.

THERE was a pool, they say, whose water clear
  Reflected everything for miles around;
And had you searched the land both far and near,
  Such sweetness elsewhere you could ne'er have
    found;
It simply was the most transparent mere
  By any mortal man beheld on ground,
And of the Water of Life such foretaste gave
As may be met with on this side the grave.

And by this pool, what time the ruddy dawn
  Saw its own face in that translucent glass,
And on the waste the fallow-deer and fawn
  Rose from their deep lair in the shaggy grass,

And the white veil of morning mist was drawn
O'er distant mountain range and craggy pass,
Two Geese were wont to plume their wings and dip
Their yellow beaks therein, and take their sip

Of Nature's finest liquor; and there too
A Tortoise dwelt, who was on closest terms
Of friendship with them, which through constant view
Of those two Geese, from first acquaintance' germs
Had ripened to affection tried and true,
(At least the chronicler thus much affirms);
And so they used to meet, and joke, and chat,
And splash and paddle on this side and that.

But after many times the circling sky
Had turned about them and the solar rays
Had slanted low or scorched them from on high,
And aged Earth had added many days
To her long life, the pool began to dry,
And frogs and water-rats, with mournful face,

Were running here and there, and giving vent
To curses on that fleeting element.

Then said those prudent Geese, with one accord,
 'This is a very awkward state of things,
And although "Change" means always "being bored,"
  And Use its halo o'er this fountain flings,
And it was sweet upon this pleasant sward
  To lie, and plume ourselves, and flap our wings,
Still we, perforce, these wonted bonds must burst,
Or else most surely we shall die of thirst.'

With looks of woe and eyes brim-full of tears,
  The sorrowing Geese to find the Tortoise went;
'Sweet friend,' quoth they, 'and neighbour now for
    years,
  With whom our happy hours have most been spent,
Since Fortune's face an evil aspect wears,
  And angry Fate is big with dark intent,

Distracted quite, we come to take our leave ;

Forgive us, friend, you know how much we grieve !

' See how our darling pond is shrinking up

    And daily showing more of weeds and mud ;

Soon there'll be nought to breakfast on or sup,

    No vestige of the bright pellucid flood

Which erst was like an ever-brimming cup

    Filled to the brim with heaven's choicest good ;

Alas ! we cannot bid the water flow,

So, ancient comrade, we must really go.'

Ah me,' replied that Tortoise slow and sad,

    Rubbing his slimy flippers in his eyes,

' If you go hence, why, I shall then go—mad,

    Thus left in solitude by old allies !

Here no society can e'er be had

    Besides yourselves, but frogs and dragon-flies ;

For water-rats are so uncommon shy,

They always hide when I am passing by.

' And if indeed the pool should disappear,
  Pray don't you know that I must die as well ?
That, like yourselves, I live in marsh and mere,
  And count the dry-land as next door to hell,
And most do love, through all the rolling year,
  In depth delicious of the flood to dwell?
Then why d' you talk such nonsense about grieving,
When me thus coolly in the lurch you're leaving?'

' Oh, dear acquaintance,' said the Geese, ' why speak
  In terms so cruel to companions old?
Why do these tears stain either's downy cheek,
  Why are we downcast, once so free and bold ?
It is because our hearts with sorrow weak
  Will hardly let our wretched plight be told,
And thrills of anguish through our bosoms shoot,
As at the parting of the web and foot.

And since 'tis evident we must depart,
  (For life is dear to everything alive)

Why do you thus unkind objections start,

    And fondly think with fate's decree to strive?

Such folly lessens not leave-taking's smart,

    But rather, more the bleeding soul doth rive ;

Say out at once what else you'd have us do;

When time is short, 'tis best that words be few.'

' I want to go with you,' the Tortoise said,

    ' Why leave me here in this waste place alone?

'Tis true I have no wings, but in their stead

    Devise me some contrivance of your own,

For you have wit and skill, in either's head

    Are brains in plenty, as to all 'tis known ;

But I have no such articles in store,

I'm a " good fellow," not an atom more.

' Alas ! that I had given to the arts

    The time I've spent in burrowing in the mud,

And had but fostered what of natural parts

    I did possess in budding babyhood ;

But now in your two sympathising hearts
  My trust is placed; to your poor friend be good,
And bear me also to some happier clime
Blessed with deep water and with deeper slime!'

The Geese replied, ''Tis true that we have notions,
  And are not wholly barren as to brain,
For we have flown o'er continents and oceans,
  And tasted many a diverse joy and pain,
And oft have drunk Experience' bitter potions,
  Whereby e'en Ignorance may wisdom gain;
And therefore, doubtless, we can well advise,
But our advice, we fear, won't make you wise.

' We have observed that you, dear gossip, are
  Somewhat to levity and "larking" given;
Forgive our mentioning this, for we are far
  From wishing to annoy you, but are driven
By candour strict to tell you, that no star
Falls half so quickly through the midnight heaven,

As you are like to do, if you should fare
Along with us through realms of empty air.

' Perhaps you've never studied gravitation ;
   Indeed your way of life has not been such
As to produce that kind of lucubration—
   A knowledge hitherto not needed much ;
But now the interests of your preservation
   That science unexplored do nearly touch,
And if you practise not by our advice,
Why—you'll be smashed to pieces in a trice.

' 'There is no doubt that if your teeth you fix
   In a strong stick of stout and seasoned oak,
And can avoid your customary tricks,
   And recollect that nothing must be spoke,
And do but hold the aforesaid stick "like bricks,"
   Nor heed at all another's gibe or joke,
We can convey you yon blue mountains o'er
To sparkling water and a pleasant shore.

' But if your head, sieve-like, our words should let

    In by the one and out of t' other ear,

And you should happen choleric to get

    At jests sarcastic you may chance to hear,

And then neglecting tight your teeth to set,

    Should answer something, down you'll tumble sheer,

Describing many a wonderful gyration

Until you land upon annihilation.

' So you must promise faithfully to keep

    Your teeth inserted in the seasoned wood,

And bid the porter of your hearing sleep

    With doors fast shut to all things, bad or good,

Until we reach that water broad and deep,

    And set you safe and sound beside the flood ;

We do not choose our friends and yours should chide,

And call us instruments of suicide.'

The Tortoise answered, 'Neighbours, you may think

    That I'm an idiot, or at least a fool,

Because I've never moved beyond the brink
   Of this much-loved but most inconstant pool,
From which, it seems, we now no more must drink ;
   But though it's true I've never been to school,
Still I can keep my mouth shut if I like,
In spite of gibing man or barking tyke.

' Bear you the stick, and I'll do all the rest ;
   My teeth will clutch it, while your beaks do hold ;
Let no misgivings either downy breast
   Afflict, but start off, confident and bold,
And e'er the sun has sunk toward the West
   And turned our harbour's azure sheet to gold,
Let us have changed dark care for smiling ease,
Couched by the sweet stream under shady trees.'

Thereat the Geese, consenting, thither brought
   A good oak plant that would not lightly bend ;
The Tortoise seized it, and as quick as thought
   The trio 'gan through yielding air ascend,

And the Geese steered toward the place they sought,
  Holding the stick that bore their daring friend,
Who, looking far from the terrestrial orb,
Determined nothing should his phlegm disturb.

But as they flew above the mountain's brow
  Just where a village hugged the brown hill-side,
As they perforce were moving somewhat slow,
  The people there that burden strange espied,
And many a fore-finger that sight did show,
  And many a cackling beldame looked and cried,
' Well, did I ever ? Wonders ne'er will cease !
To see a Tortoise carried by two Geese !'

The Tortoise's bile began to rise at this,
  He longed to meet these taunts with repartee ;
Thought he, ' The Geese at least might give a hiss,
  To show how we despise their contumely ;
Oh, that I now could bite each withered Miss
  Who dares let fly her sarcasm at me !'

Then as his wrath his recollection passes,
He thus begins rejoinder, 'Dolts and asses——'

At once attraction did its force assert;
　His head went down, up flew his nether parts;
No more he utters of his answer pert,
　With headlong speed towards the earth he darts—
Now, crushed and pounded, mixed with stone and
　　dirt,
　His shapeless body warns unstable hearts
To hold their way through ridicule and blame,
And learn to be, in either, still the same.

HOW THE HUSBAND OF TWO WIVES
LOST HIS BEARD.

THE beard of an elderly merchant, they say,
    Resembled the time twixt the day and the night,
Or if you prefer it, the night and the day;
    That is, some hairs were black and the others were
        white.

In early life he had married a wife
    Of about the same years as himself, and now
Age's wintry finger, that will not linger,
    Had frosted the scanty thatch on her old 'pow.'

Inconstant man's frail thoughts *will* rove
    From the ugly and old to the pretty and young;
And small is the empire of constant love,
    In spite of the fine things that poets have sung.

So that merchant has ta'en him a juvenile spouse
With a tulip cheek and a sparkling eye;
But intent upon peace and a quiet house,
He treated them both most impartially.

He said in his heart, 'They shall live apart,
And in regular order I'll visit them both;
And thus their collusion can't breed confusion,
Nor jealousy sting them, I'll take my oath.

'I will act to both quite as is lawful and right;
Of favouring either I've no idea;
And care I'll take that neither shall make
The complaint that was made against Rachel by
Leah.'

So if one day he went and the evening spent
With his last married fair one, the next he would go
And do the same with the ancient dame,
That the stream of existence might peaceably flow.

Now after dinner, this shocking old sinner

    (At least he'll be thought so, I fear, in the West),

Was wont to lay down his grizzled crown

    On the sofa cushions, and take a short rest.

One evening he'd set up his usual snore,

    After taking a snack with his elderly wife,

When she thought to herself, ' 'Tis a terrible bore

    That my husband lives with me but half his life !

' How happy we were ere that nasty creature

    Came spoiling the sweets of our conjugal bliss !

A hideous wretch, too ! without a feature

    That a tom-cat would think it worth while to kiss !

' If I *could* but find some plan to my mind

    That would draw him at once and for ever to me,

That here he might stay both night and day,

    At breakfast and luncheon, at dinner and tea !'

Thus thinking, the place of her husband's repose,

    With cat-like footstep she stealthily neared,

And admiringly gazed at his short snub nose,

    And his mouth so capacious, half hid by his beard.

As she stood in thought, her fancy caught

    A bright inspiration from that very beard,

Where in spite, as was said, of his being twice wed,

    A great many black hairs still appeared.

'Aha ! said she, 'I imagine I see

    The way to manage this little affair !

This once I will steal a device from Dalila,

    And capture my Samson by means of his hair !

'Those black things I'll grub out and carefully rub out

    All signs of youth from my husband's face,

His beard shall be white, which to youthful sight

    Is a blemish far worse than the blot of disgrace.

K

'So in time I shall manage to make that slut
 Take a perfect disgust to my sweet poppet here,
And thus betwixt *them* shall establish a "cut,"
 And I shall be thenceforth his only dear!'

Then cautiously grabbing his beard, she 'gan stabbing
 It through with the tweezers in every spot,
And with many a pull she did gingerly cull
 About half the black hairs her poor husband had
  got.

The very next day he went to pay
 His wonted respects to the younger spouse ;
After 'pegs' a good number, in grateful slumber,
 He was giving a concert of bullocks and sows :

Now this lady's opinions were caught from the
  moderns,
 And therefore she stickled for fashion and rule,

(As a poor man we see who his bread with a hod
  earns
More polished than noblemen of the old school) :

So hearing this rumpus unearthly, she thought,
  'What a terrible Goth my dear husband's been
    made !
'Tis that old harridan to this pickle has brought
  His manners ; the twopence she cannot have paid !

'This grunting and wheezing is very unpleasing ;
  But how shall I manage his errors to cure ?
If I scold him to-day, when he goes away,
  To-morrow that hag to encourage is sure !

'It never will do, that is certain, to let her
  Thus poison his mind with her old-fashioned ways.
I somehow must manage to make him forget her,
  And pass with me only the rest of his days '

K 2

Then quietly creeping to where he lay sleeping,
    She looked on his features with thoughtful eye ;
She examined the hair of his beard, and there
    Was astonished so many white bristles to spy.

' Aha !' said she, ' I can plainly see
    The only way to manage the thing ;
I will instantly pluck these hairs, my duck,
    From your beard, till it's black as a raven's wing !

' Then you'll look twice as young as you did before,
    And therefore will naturally turn to me,
And will send, I trust, that withered old—bore
    To—, the place where she really deserves to
      be !'

Then she narrowly peered through all parts of his
      beard,
    And pulled out as many white hairs as she could ;
So I think it is plain, that between the twain,
    A thinness ensued in that bristly wood.

When back he came to the elderly dame,

    She inspected his hirsute appendage anew,

And, much amazed as thereon she gazed,

    Thought, 'Why what on earth has been done to
        you?

· I fancied I'd pulled the black hairs out clean,

    But now more than ever offend my sight;

What can it all mean?   He can't have been

    And dyed it?   Oh no! for I see *some* white.

'However, it's clear, if I still persevere,

    In time I am sure to produce an effect;

It must also be reckoned that Age *will* second

    These efforts, that something untoward has
        checked.'

While thus moralizing, she set to work prising

    Out all the black hairs with a praiseworthy zeal,

And did so redouble attacks on that stubble,
  That it soon looked as white as a fresh willow-
    peel.

Ah ! why tell the tale how the younger female
  Waged war to the knife on those white hairs
    again ?
How that beard full of bristles, as stiff as a thistle's,
  With the waning moon each night continued to
    wane !

Till sunk in thought, that merchant sought
  One day, as he pondered, his beard to pull ;
Oh how he did stare !   There was never a hair
  Of that forest that once was so thick and so full !

He bellowed and swore—but why tell any more ?
  And of prosy moral pray what is the need ?
To the world I leave it—who does not perceive it
  Is certain to meet with a similar meed !

THE REWARD OF THE ARCHITECT OF KHAWAMAK.[1]

KHAWAMAK palace is goodly to see,
Low in the river or high on the lea;
From north and south and west and east
Alike, to the eye 'tis a royal feast :

 Nothing there
 Looks ugly or bare—
All is marvellous, all is fair :
From the vast central dome, all set
 With richest fretting round,
And ringed by many a minaret
 With wondrous carving crowned,

---

[1] Built in Babylonia.

To every single stone,
No curious glance of architect
Can one minutest flaw detect,
    Save this, perchance, alone,
That such perfection ne'er before
In city, desert, hill, or shore
    By eye of mortal seen,
Would seem to show it owed its birth
To no skilled hand of middle earth,
But rather Iram's vanished bower
Had there been brought in magic hour
    And planted on that green.

And sure no necromancer's hall
    Deep down beneath the Kulgum Sea,
No palace girt with diamond wall
    On storied Mount of Tartary,
E'er shone so bright, both noon and night,
With ever-varying coloured light,

That needed not the sun or moon :

It was light-music played in tune ;

A giant prism, where each hue

Now plain was seen, now lost to view ;

Now, like a beam of morning sun,

The colours melted into one ;

Anon, in separate sheen disclose

The sapphire, emerald, and rose.

And all around those brilliant walls

   A garden spread, whose bright parterres

   Were such as in no halting verse

Could e'er be painted ; waterfalls

   And sparkling fountains dashed and played

For ever in those lovely bowers

Where, loath to part, the enamoured Hours.

   Neglectful of Time's march, delayed.

The box-tree and the cedar bowed

   In the soft wind that, breathing spice,

Blew gently o'er that Paradise
   The much-reluctant fleecy cloud.
And in the centre of the alleys green
   That to the wild-wood branched this way and that,
There was a rose-garden, the finest seen
   In any clime at any time ; one flat
Of desert sand it had been, bare and lone,
Scorched by the wind ; no single plant had grown
Upon its tawny breast since Adam fell ;
Though here, some held, was once the deepest dell
   Of happy Eden, when its flowers and trees
Bloomed fairest, fostered by the genial spell
   Of Peace unbroken ; and the amorous breeze
Touched the sweet cheek that had not learned to
    grieve,
And waved the tresses of untempted Eve.

The beauties of those roses who can tell ?
   Not those who saw them ; why then how should I,

Or any man who writes ten times as well,
    Unfold their charms with strict veracity?
'Tis well the Roman of the Pæstum beds
    Should sing with rapture, and that Hafiz too
Should praise the blossoms wound round Sheeráz
       heads,
    Or I should speak of Sydenham and Kew,
Or any soul should talk of what it knows;
But who shall dare to paint Khawamak's rose?

Suffice it, then, that from the sandy plain
    Genius had conjured up that place renowned,
Proceeding from the ever-toiling brain
    Of the then greatest architect on ground,
Who now stands pondering in an alley lone
    On well-earned meed for that vast labour done.
'Twas Sinimmar that garden-palace wrought,
And wrapped in train of dear delusive thought,
He plucks a flower, as they are wont who muse,
And o'er the walk its purple petals strews.

Soft to himself he says, ' What work like this ?

What minarets like those the skies do kiss ?

   Who else could make

   Yon lily-sprinkled lake,

Yon leaping fountains, and yon shady bowers,

This wealth of starlike flowers,

Out of the herbless, hardly-trodden waste,

Far from sown field and walléd city placed ?

Not Eden, sacred dwelling-place of bliss,

Could e'er have been more beautiful than this ?

' For this my brain, both night and day,

Not knowing rest, has thought and toiled alway.

And now at last the fruit I reap,

All is accomplished, and my brain may sleep :

But what the meed of my reflection deep

   And constant wakefulness for many years ?

To what strange height of honour shall I leap, —

   What undreamed greatness, far above my peers ?

' Will they open the hoard,

  Got with cursing and tears,

  Gathered and stored

  In Hira for years,

Wool that was shorn from that sheep, the people,

  with bloody shears?

' Or in the wide hall

  Of the Takht-i-Jamsheed [1]

  My name will they call,

  And my steps will they lead

To the throne of King Bahram the hunter, the lover

  of hound and of steed ?

' Will he bid them array me

  In purple and gold,

  On his own horse convey me

  Through city and wold,

That o'er all the broad empire of Iran the tale of my

  glory be told ?

     [1] Persepolis.

' Or else it may be

That dominion and power

Will be granted to me

Over Gobar and Gour,

And a line of the nobles of Ajam may spring into

birth from that hour.

' And my children will ride

With their feudal array

Where the leaders of Pride

Square the ranks for the fray,

And the banner of Kas[1] o'er the dust and the din

of mid-battle doth sway.

' Let them do as they will,

And reward as they may,

[1] The ancient banner of Persia, said to be the apron of the
blacksmith Kas, the conqueror of Zohak.

A debt to me still
    Must be owing alway,
For never the guerdons of Power the wages of Genius
    can pay.'

    Hira's King is sitting high
        Upon Hira's throne,
    Councillors are standing by,
        Nobles many a one ;
    Their speech is of that mighty pile
        That Sinimmar had raised,
    Size, and ornament, and style,
        Everything they praised :
    Such a work and such a man
    Was not since the world began !

    N'umán the King sits still and listens,
    Now and then his dark eye glistens,
        Not a word says he,

But his hand, his robe beneath,
Trifles with his dagger-sheath
  Somewhat curiously.

He was never given to prating,
And he sits there silent, waiting
  Till they all have done;
Then says, 'Now I recollect,
I must see this architect—
  Send him here alone!'

*   *   *   *

Sinimmar is bowing low
  Before Hira's throne,
Whereon N'umán, dark of brow,
  Sitteth all alone;
There no single page doth wait,
All must stand without the gate.
'Builder,' said the king at length,
  All your work do praise,

Monument of skill and strength
   Till the latest days.
Let, they say, the force of nations
Try to sap those deep foundations,
They shall ne'er prevail;
Rooted they as hell infernal,
And the towers, like heaven supernal,
Will not sink or fail.
Yet. I hear, there is a boulder
   In that palace wall
That, if pushed by stalwart shoulder,
   Straightway down will fall;
And the castle then will totter,
Heave and burst, and ruin utter
   Will demolish all.
Tell me, is this false or true—
Do any know that stone but you?'

Sinimmar replied, 'O king!
Science is a wondrous thing;

You who, loving only war,
Snuff the battle from afar,
Who from earliest spring of years
See but flash of swords and spears,
Hold all men of little worth
Save the conquerors of earth;
But to mortals such as we,
Armed with mighty alchemy,
Peace gives fairer victory;
While her golden wand she waves,
We can subjugate *our* slaves,
Push our arms of temper rare
Through the ocean, fire, and air,
Make the Powers of Matter yield,
Inch by inch, the bloodless field!

'Those halls majestic that my hand has built,
The adamantine walls, the massy towers,
The floors and ceilings fretted, carved, and gilt,
The bosky labyrinth of woods and flowers,

These are a triumph of the eternal mind,

Where Chaos reigned before, and Ruin stalks behind !

'That stone, O king, no eyes but mine have seen,

    For 'twas I placed it, as consummate Art

Has taught me ; it is small, and rough, and mean.

    And has no beauty in its outer part ;

Yet all the structure on that stone depends,—

With it, shines on for aye, without it, instant ends !'

''Tis well,' the king said, 'bid all men come in,

    And you your great reward shall straightway know.'

Then chiefs and nobles entered with a din,

    And stood expectant the high throne below :

And smiling with a cold sardonic smile,

King N'umán pondered for a little while.

'Subjects and slaves,' quoth he, 'all present here,

    Myself included, Persia's king revere ;

For him Khawamak's turrets touch the skies,
For him was formed that flowery Paradise ;
And since we hold him highest potentate
Of all the earth, and greatest of the great,
We must be careful that no other king
A fairer palace should to being bring,
And mock our efforts with more heavenly flowers,
A more abiding pleasure-house than ours.
We must guard too 'gainst finger of Decay
That else might steal our joy and boast away :
The secret place of the all-mining stone
Is patent to the master-mind alone.
How vast a mind that down that pile could fling
By trifling pressure on so small a thing !
Admire the architect, most justly too ;
But I just now have something more to do !
Take, slaves, the builder to the topmost tower,
Let him look well o'er garden, lake, and bower,
'Tis his reward ; his great work let him see,
Then hurl him downward to Eternity !

So shall that castle stand unmatched, alone,

And none be wiser for the hidden stone ! '

And this was the Reward of Sinimmar,

Who carried skill miraculous too far !

HOW THE CROWS CAME TO BE BLACK, AND THE HOOPOES TO HAVE CROWNS ON THEIR HEADS.

KING Solomon's off to the furthest West,

He is fond of travel and never can rest;

    But he has no need

    Of mortal steed

Whatever its blood, or whatever its breed ;

    He wants no train

    Of mortal strain

Pages and nobles at home remain ;

    His horse is the throne

    That he sits upon,

By men unattended, but not alone ;

    For everywhere

To him repair

The birds and the Jinns and the Powers of the Air !

That golden throne moves steadily on

From the break of dawn till the day is done ;

With a favouring wind it steers aright

Without a pause, through the starry night ;

Above the earth it holds its way,

Without a let, with never a stay,

With no desire for corn or hay ;

It has no tricks,

It never kicks.

And is not driven by spurs or sticks ;

No startling sight it passes by

Can ever make it jib or shy ;

'Tis better than a steam-engine,

Because it goes without a line,

'Tis better than the ' Monstre ' balloon,

For it can visit the sun and moon ;

And so, no doubt, King Solomon thinks
As he sits thereon, and winks and blinks.

.

Why should the eyes of King Solomon wink,
And why should he turn uneasilie,
As though the silk of his cushions pink
Had dared to harbour a rebel flea?
The fact is that the sun is burning,
And the king keeps this and that way turning,
To look for a bird, or a demon, or sprite,
Who will fly 'twixt his head and the source of light.
He says to himself, 'Why didn't I tell a
Fairy to bring my green umbrella?
I think I must have left it standing
Upon the first or second landing,
When I returned from the tea-party,
Given by the fair Astarte;
Or stay—'twas leaning 'gainst the door,
Upon Salome's second floor—

The Crows and the Hoopoes.

No, no—I left it at the gate
The day of Pharaoh's daughter's fête—
· Then where's the ticket?—But hallo!
Come here, you flying there, you crow!'

It happened that a flight of crows
Were passing by the monarch's nose
   In orderly array;
Not dressed, as now, in plumage dark,
With voice as hoarse as bloodhound's bark,
   But dappled like the day,
When through light clouds and summer air
It rises, Phœbus' harbinger;
And having voices mild and soft
As August wind through orchard croft;
   No birds more fair than they,
None woke a softer melody
From wind-rocked nest in old elm tree;
Nought then was heard of dismal 'caw,'
The burden now of corvine 'jaw!'

'Come here,' again that great king said,

'And shade my scorchéd eyes and head ;

This heat is really past a joke,

I fear that I shall get a " stroke ;"

So come and fly above my poll,

And act the part of parasol !'

' O puissant king !' their chief replied,

And for a moment turned aside,

' Forgive if in laconic style

I answer you ; to Britain's isle

In headlong haste we now are bound

(It is the sweetest spot on ground)

To settle in a certain wood

That hangs o'er Avon's lovely flood,

And if we should delay,

Some other feathered tribe would seize

The feathery tops of those fair trees,

And rocked to sleep by ocean breeze

In twig-bound nest would sway.

On others lay your high commands ;
Adieu, great prince ! we kiss your hands.'
Then turning from the astonished king,
The crow flew off on lightning wing.

' By Balaam's ass !' King Solomon exclaimed,
(The whole throne trembled when that oath was
named)
' Such barefaced impudence was never seen
Since misty vapour first made all things green !
Don't they know I'm the lord
Of the flaming sword,
And the diamond breastplate that can't be bored,
And the shield that was forged by Ján bin Ján
Ages before there was ever a man ?
Do they want to feel
The powers of my seal ?
They *shall*, or I'll take me a sceptre of deal !
And so, here goes, for better for worse ;
Look out, other people, I'm going to curse !

' Every man jack

    Of a crow shall be black

On his head and his breast and his wings and his back,

    And shall lose his sweet voice,

    And utter a noise

To be mimicked by pert little girls and boys,

    Hoarse and harsh,

    Worse than frogs in a marsh,

Or the creaking that issues from juvenile toys ;

    And every old crone,

    All skin and bone,

Whose nose and chin are nearly one,

And whose back is curved like a bended bow

Shall be said to resemble an agéd crow !

    When the farmers sow,

    And the seed doesn't grow.

All shall be laid to the door of the crow !

Sticks and clods they all shall throw,

    Twang shall go

    The deadly cross-bow.

Ping ! ping !

The stone from the sling ;

And when the sun

Some ages has run,

Bang shall go the fowler's gun ;

Every one of them fraught with woe

Wounds and death to the wretched crow ! '

When that fiat left the royal mouth,

East and west, and north, and south,

    Everywhere

    Through earth and air,

The winds and the Jinns the news did bear ;

    Every young crow

    Who in accents low

Was pleading his suit beneath the nest

Of the shy modest fair one he loved the best,

Found to his horror, surprise, and awe,

That his love-notes changed to a hideous 'caw !'

And his mistress almost fainted with fright,

When she found herself minus her feathers white,

And hoarsely crying, 'Alas ! Alack !'

Observed that her wings and her breast and her back

Resembled the 'Gentleman dressed in black !'

The sun keeps on getting higher and higher

Till it scorches King Solomon's brain like fire ;

There's never a cloud in the clear blue sky

To serve as a shade and canopy ;

The king exclaims, 'How I envy the shiver

Of houseless beggars in wintry cold !

How I wish I were one of the fish in the river,

And that somebody else had my throne of gold !

    But stay, but stay—

    What's flying this way?

Is it a pigeon, or jackdaw, or jay ?

No, no, by the pokers, here's my man,

The King of the Hoopoes, and all his clan !

    Hallo ! I say !—

    How d'ye do ? Good day !

Just please to come and fly this way,

Or the heat my skin from my body will flay !'

The hoopoes were a cheerful race,

Somewhat bald as to head and face,

But largely possessed of Civility's grace :

And as soon as they saw the state of the case,

They came 'twixt the king and the burning rays.

With a sigh of relief, King Solomon now

Wipes the drops from his lofty brow,

Which looks a little peeled and brown

From the ardent looks the sun shot down ;

And he has ta'en off his jewelled crown,

And begun to smile and ceased to frown ;

And presently, fanned by the hoopoes' wings

Has lost recollection of mundane things,

And sinking down in the cushions deep

Is 'taking it out' in a pleasant sleep.

O'er tower and tree,

Lawn and lea,

Yellow sand and emerald sea,

The throne flew on unceasingly,

Till the ridge of Káf, the utmost bound

Of all the world, before it frowned ;

From inky clefts resounds the flow

Of the torrents that pour from the upper snow,

Snow that glitters cold and white

From many a lone untrodden height ;

And on the topmost pointed spire

Is the beacon red of eternal fire.

Pity it is, from modern sight,

That famous peak has vanished quite

That once was real, through the East,

For peer and prophet, prince and priest ;

Vision for ages cherished long

By lay and legend, text and song,

A pageant, in this wiser day,

Swept by the 'march of mind' away !

But then, no pincushion so full of pins,

As was Mount Káf of Fairies, Divs, and Jinns !

Knowing the king was to this harbour bound,

The throne descended softly to the ground,

With just so much of a gentle bump

As made its master from slumber jump ;

He stared in surprise,

Rubbed his eyes,

Looked at the mountain, the throne, and the skies,

And said as he gazed at the towering steep,

' I really think I have been asleep ! '

But when he saw the heaven flecked

With the myriads of his train,

He began the matter to recollect,

So stretched and yawned, and commenced to reflect

That the King of the Hoopoes would doubtless expect

Some recompense to gain

For having thus travelled o'er land and main

Merely to act as a covering, or veil,

To preserve Solomon from a *coup de soleil.*

So he said to that complaisant potentate,

' Be so kind as to wait

M

A moment, for though it must be rather late,

You'll excuse me, I hope, if I keep you a second

While my debt to your kindness is being reckoned;

    Let me see, let me see—

    What is your fee

For attending upon me so courteously ?

Don't be afraid to mention your price,

My treasurer here will " shell out " in a trice !

Or if you're afraid that because I'm a Jew

I may try to cheat you out of your due,

Instead of hard cash make you take a few

Rickety chairs and a picture or two,

With a grand piano " almost new,"

Etcetera, pray take the trouble to choose

Yourself what you'd like, and I won't refuse ;

    A carte-blanche fill

    In as you will ;

Write what you like, and I'll honour the bill !'

' Lord of the Seal,' the hoopoe prince replied,

' To do your bidding is our joy and pride ;

And for reward—well, since you are so kind.

I'll tell you what I—No, no, never mind—

I think we all should—Stop though, that won't do—

Your majesty perhaps a day or two

Will grant me, just to talk the matter over

With my dear wife, who, greatly as I love her.

And she me too, of course, is sometimes taken

    With tears, hysterics, and perhaps a fit,

And then the nest gets disagreeably shaken,

    And I and every one fall out of it,

And the unfledged princesses in the dirt

Drop headlong down, and now and then are hurt.

I think, in order to avoid a scene,

    I'd better ask her first what she would like,

You best must know that woman's wit is keen—

    Rather too keen if angrily it strike ;

I think she's sure to fix on something nice,

And anyhow I *must* take her advice.

Doubtless your majesty, with all your learning

    And wisdom, finds it lively at odd times,

When one of your sultanas' wrath is burning,

  To have to listen to the various chimes

Rung out by brass-like clapper of her tongue

In discord never to be said or sung !'

The great King Solomon hung his head,

With a sigh and a sheepish look, and said,

' Yes, yes, 'tis a reasonable request,

  And I wish her counsel may be for the best :

So off with you to your royal nest,

And when you have the whole confessed

To your spouse, bring me her high behest ;

I will endeavour her highness to please,

And the wheels of your conjugal cart to grease.

I shall be back in Jerusalem town

To-morrow, before the sun goes down ;

But now to the summit of Káf I must go,

To chat with the Simurgh[1] among the snow.'

---

[1] Sovereign of the birds.

Round Jerusalem town
The mountains brown
Are changed into blue as the sun goes down ;
A golden speck is resting yet
On wooded brow of Olivet ;
Though every moment up the hill
The evening shade creeps higher still ;
Hushed is the lonely wood-bird's trill,
But softly murmurs Kedron's rill ;
No sound beside invades the calm,
And listless droops the giant palm.

But there on high,
In the purple sky,
What flashes broad and bright ?
'Tis some flying thing,
Yet has never a wing,
And it looks too large for a kite ;
And now it glides o'er the sacred wall
That girds Jerusalem's city tall,

And now, in the palace of David's son,
'Tis lost; long live great Solomon !

The golden throne in the palace square
Descended from the upper air ;
   When the king looked round
   There on the ground,
With a loyal smile and a bow profound,
The hoopoe monarch in waiting he found.
   ' Well,' said the king,
   You're quick on the wing !
   How's the queen?
   Did she ask where you'd been
   And what you had seen,
   And what you could mean
By daring to loiter so long away
From her, when she'd told you not to stay ?
   Never mind, never mind !
   Such remarks are unkind—
We all have our trials—at least, so *I* find !

So now just tell me what you want :
'Tis yours to ask, and mine to grant !'

' My liege,' replied the hoopoe-king,
' Honey is made by bees that sting ;
The fairest rose has got a thorn ;
The night's good liquor bites at morn.
I have a wife ; and so, you know,
I have my hours of joy and woe ;
But to your grace it does not matter
Whether the former or the latter
Predominate ; but you can guess ;
Such things who dare in words express?
My wife her heart hath wholly set
Upon a golden coronet
By every hoopoe to be worn.
She says, she hears that constant scorn,
Improper mocks, and heartless jests,
Attend our somewhat scanty crests ;

And she opines a lady's head,

At least, should be well-covered.

Thus I, O king ! will make so bold

As to request that crowns of gold

May shine on every hoopoe's head,

This "pitiful bald crown" instead !'

King Solomon paused for a little while,

And regarded his friend with a curious smile :

    ' Ah,' said he, ' now I see

That one is as bad as three hundred times three.

      Indeed I believe

      That men will perceive,

In time, what a fine thing is plurality !

A husband's unlikely to be led away

By what, 'mid a hundred, a unit may say ;

      But with only *one*,

      It's as clear as the sun,

That he cannot avoid being thoroughly done !

Now, my dear hoopoe,

I'm grateful to you

For the excellent service you happened to do ;

So I'll give you a piece of counsel true ;—

Though stay, stay—

Why throw away

Pearls upon—that is, I mean to say—

You shall all have gold crowns, glittering and gay,

And yet not a single farthing to pay !

But there'll be Someone else to—however, look here !

If at last you find

Your crown not to your mind,

Have no fear ;

Hitherward steer,

And pour your griefs in my friendly ear !'

The hoopoe-king from the presence has flown,

Not quite certain whether his own

Or some other person's head stands on his

shoulders,

So very weighty 't has suddenly grown ;

And in the palace-yard all beholders

> Stare at the skies

> Through which he flies,

And, with mouths wide open, remark, ' My eyes !'

All over Judah and Israel

There wasn't a river or fountain or well

Or bright little pool set in forest green,

Whereat a hoopoe was not to be seen,

With all its soul admiring the sheen

Of its golden crown, and with haughty mien,

Turning its head this way and that.

Like an East-end clerk in a West-end hat ;

Now, with its beak turned up in the air,

Winking knowingly at the broad glare

Of noon, as much as to say, ' You up there

Are all very well ; but how you do stare

> At *me !*

> Now you see

A glory with which you can *not* compare !'
And then perhaps on the brink it stood,

    Bending down,

    Its flaming crown,

To see if it couldn't set fire to the flood !
In short, it practised a select assortment
Of all the choicest antics of ' deportment.'

    By evil hap,

    One day in a trap,

A fowler (anything but an ass)
Instead of corn put a looking-glass,
And an orphan hoopoe, young, untaught,
Wrapped up in self-admiring thought,
By its own countenance was caught.
   The fowler came to take his prey,

    But when he saw its head

   Set in a crown so bright and gay,
Quite taken aback, he had nothing to say,

    But ' I'm ——,' well, never mind what he said ;

'Twas a very expressive Hebrew oath,

Which to translate I'm something loath.

The cap of pride soon all must doff—

In half a shake that crown was off !

And the fowler's off to the great bazaar,

To the shop of an old merchant named Issachar,

Who was as cunning as cunning can be

In the very *arcana* of metallurgy ;

    The fowler laid down

    That golden crown

Before Issachar, who, with smile and frown,

And many a hitch of his greasy gown,

Felt it on this side, and smelt it on that,

Much in the way that a cautious cat

Sniffs an apparently dead mouse or rat ;

And then he got out his scales and weights,

And weighed it as though on its value the fates

Of Judah and Israel and all states

From Euphrates' river, to Gaza's gates,

Must depend,

Till the world should end;

And the fowler in silence his *dictum* awaits.

Quotes Issachar, with that wonderful leer,

Which so universally's seen to appear

On the Hebrew ' mug,' when engaged in trading,

Meant to be pleading and also persuading—

' Well now, this *is* pretty!

In all the city

A sweeter thing is not to be found,

So nicely shaped and so perfectly round !

But then you see,

To a man like me,

Ornament's not solidity ;

This is very well-gilt—there isn't a doubt ;

But want of reality's soon found out ;

With a regular goldsmith it never would pass

For anything more than a crown of brass !

But though trade is so bad

That we're all going mad,

I wish to be liberal, especially to you,

Whose face is so open and honest and true.

To be other than generous is always amiss,

So I'll give you a shekel of silver for this !

If you catch any more, you know, bring them to me.

I shall always treat you handsomely !'

When next the fowler a hoopoe caught,

With its crown in his hand the old merchant he sought;

But on his way thither he happened to meet

With a goldsmith who lived in the selfsame street,

   Who called to him, 'Stop !

What's that you are taking to Issachar's shop?

I saw you go there once before ;

Whoever enters that old villain's door

Is sure to be done completely brown ;

What is it you've got?   Oh, I see, a crown—

    And by Joshua it's gold !

    Stay, let me hold

It a moment ; yes, yes, and for what have you sold

The other you took to old Issachar's shop?

For cash, or for something by way of a swop?

A shekel of silver? Come, come, pooh, pooh!

Honour bright? well, that *was* a regular do!

    Of course 'tis true

    That every Jew

Likes a bit of a profit, but really that's too

Much of a good thing; He! he! he!

A shekel of silver! Now just hear me;

I'm ready to pay you, properly told,

And down on the nail, a full talent of gold!'

      *   *   *   *   *

From Lebanon white to the lone Dead Sea,

    By mountain and by flood,

In hilly Judæa and flat Galilee,

    In desert and in wood,

Nothing is heard but the twang of the string

As through strident air the arrows sing,

    And the stone's sharp ping

From the whirling sling

After every hoopoe seen on the wing !

For as to sitting, *that* wasn't a thing

That any one of them could venture to do ;

For as sure as he did so, he fell, pierced through

By several stones and an arrow or two,

While from every bush rushed an eager Hebrew

Yelling, ' My bird ! *I* killed him ! *You* let him alone !

Just look at the mark of my arrow (or stone)?'

So at last the poor king,

Completely worn out by this kind of thing,

Resolved to return to Jerusalem town,

And beg Solomon to take off the gold crown !

　　At dead of night

　　Did the hoopoe alight

At Solomon's window, much more like a sprite

Than a bird, and that prince, in a deuce of a fright,

　　Commenced to recite

A long exorcism, of marvellous might,

Enough to turn Belial's blue beard white ;

But his visitor having no time to delay,

And in mortal terror of coming day,

Managed to smash a pane in two,

And with some loss of feathers, to scramble through.

    With obeisance meet

      He fell at the feet

Of the Lord of the Seal, who was pleased to greet

His friend, when he saw who it was had got in ;

And chucking him pleasantly under the chin,

      Said, ' You needn't begin ;

You've found that your queen made a slight mistake,

And from dreams of her wisdom you're now wide awake;

And you've flown here at this most unearthly hour

To ask me to make a slight stretch of my power,

      And be pleased to lift

      My dangerous gift

From your heads, while you've got any heads at all ;

But listen ; I cannot entirely recall

That precious boon

You've tired of so soon ;

But this much I'll do

Out of kindness to you :

Your heads shall be sore

With that weight no more,

And your crowns shall be thatched now with feathers,

not ore !

And please to remember these parting words—

Fine feathers don't always make fine birds !'

HOW THE KING OF KHURÁSÁN WAS CURED OF THE RHEUMATISM.

KHURÁSÁN is a sunny land,
  As its name, it is thought, implies;
And its soil is possessed of a good deal of sand,
  And its air of some rather large flies;
But what does that matter to me or to you?
Our affair's with its puissant king, Mansoor bin Nuh.

Mansoor bin Nuh is ill at ease,
But not from the sand, or the flies, or the fleas;
Oh no! He is too much accustomed to these.
Though the sun without is scorching and baking,
Within the poor king sits, shivering and shaking,
And his limbs are all stiff, and his joints are all aching

He can't find out

What it's all about,

And the pain makes him sometimes inclined to shout.

And the doctors stare

At the king in his chair. ;

They pinch him here and they poke him there,

In heart and liver, in lungs and wind,

Before and behind ;

They assault him with medicines of every kind,

Till he's very nearly out of his mind.

But alas ! no relief from that pain can he find !

Hakeem Akbar Ali says, if he will take

A mixture composed of the skin of a snake,

And the web of one foot of a Brahmany drake,

And the tail and the fins and perhaps a flake

From the back of a fish from the Níshapin lake

That, by help of these articles,

The phlegmatic particles

That the mucous membrane

Had secreted, and pain

Had thus ensued, would at once collapse,

And his majesty would be relieved—perhaps !

Tabeeb Abu Nasar with scorn replies,

With uplifted hands and upturned eyes,

   ' If the king (may he reign

     For ever !) would deign

To listen awhile to the children of Science,

And in pompous pretenders place no reliance,

    There isn't a doubt

    We shall soon rout out

This accursed complaint from his person sublime.

And he will be right as a trivet—in time !'

He then proceeded, with unction and gravity,

To discourse at some length on the cerebral cavity,

The abdominal tissues, the functions of food,

And the stamina gained by absorption of wood :

' Let the king,' said he, ' take a seat facing the south,

  With a pipe in his nostril instead of his mouth,

  And for several hours inhale the smoke

  Of fir, assafœtida, pine, and bog-oak,

  And a marvellous change we soon shall see

  In the powers of the royal vitality!'

And this was the way, the livelong day,

The embattled doctors hammered away,

And screamed their own renderings of Plato and

    Socrates,

Filings from Galen, and scraps from Hippocrates,

    Till the king, in despair,

    No more could bear,

But roared in a tone would have gratified Grattan,

' Get out, you d—d, humbugging, uncles of Satan !'

Then his majesty summoned the Pillars of State,

And the Eyes of the Presence, to high debate.

Said he, ' My lords, I tell you what, do you know

(Concealment is useless), this *is* a nice go !

I can scarcely refrain from curses and stamps,

I'm so racked with aches and twisted with cramps !

    Then the doctors too !

    They do nothing but brew

Such fearful decoctions, they've turned my beard blue!

There's simply not one of them worth a sou,

So I really can't tell what to do !'

Then one of the Oomara, a sensible man,

Gave a hitch to his trowsers, and thus began :

' Peace to the king !   Though how that can be

With these spalpeens of doctors, I really don't see !

    And the slicing off heads,

    Though it sometimes leads

To greater clearness in those that remain,

Will certainly not soothe your majesty's pain !

    And although the climate of Khurásán,

    And its soil, are possessed of the needful appliances

That go towards making an average man,

Yet they don't seem to foster the medical sciences.

 Now, if you should care

 To hunt elsewhere

For a doctor to whom king and kaiser repair,

 The man that I

 Should advise you to try

Is Meerza Muhammad Zákiria of Rei !'

Mansoor bin Nuh with delight cut a caper,

Cried, ' He is the cove !' and demanded some paper :

Then composed an epistle, a trifle short,

(For literary labours were not his ' forte ')

To the sage above-mentioned, to this effect :

' Your speedy attendance we daily expect !

 So take our advice,

 Be here in a trice ;

And if you don't cure us of all our ills,

You shall swallow a box of your Purgative Pills !'

Not doubting that *savant* renowned to inveigle

With this invitation, so wholly *en règle,*

The king to that ameer said, ' Now, sir, I want you

To instantly pack up your private portmanteau,

    And, without delay,

    To hasten away,

    And by no means to stay

    At any inn, pothouse, or *car'vanserai,*[1]

But encourage your horse with crack and whack

On his head and his tail and his sides and his
back,

As though Charles of the Hammer were hard on
your track ;

And although this treatment may disagree

With your steed's constitution, why, don't you see,

It's no matter—you're doing it all for *me !*

So off with you,—That 'll do !—Ta-ta !—Good-by !

Take this letter and ride like old Harry to Rei !''

---

[1] So pronounced and spelt in the East.

Muhammad Zákiria sits moody and lone,

Wife nor chick nor child he hath none,

Alas ! they are under the cold grey stone.

For he was so wedded to frequent reflection

On some new elixir, drug, pill, or confection,

That constantly stewing, and boiling, and brewing

Made him sometimes forgetful of what he was doing ;

So after a day's scientific experiment

On root and on herb and on leaf and on berry,
    blent

With various members of cat and dog, rat and frog,

And with everything down in the chemical catalogue,
    He would often doubt
    How his brews would turn out,

Having got a remarkably shady notion

Of how he had mixed each particular potion ;

So when he'd used up every monkey and rabbit

In the country around, he contracted a habit

Of making experiments his wife and his boys on,

To see if a compound were cordial or poison !

Thus one by one, in a little time,

They all, in the interests of science sublime,

Met with 'extinction of animation,'

Martyrs to medical investigation !

    Indeed, one day,

    So people say,

Muhammad Zákiria was heard to avow

That he often wished, *now,*

That he'd not fallen out with his mother-in-law,

Who, in spite of the wonderful flow of her 'jaw,'

Was an excellent person for trying a 'test' on,

On account of her marvellous powers of digestion !

    Howe'er that may be,

    'Tis nothing to me;

    I repeat that he

Was sitting alone in his surgery,

Having just dissected by aid of a spoon, his

Most recent subject, a 'pulex communis,'

(Or, as some antiquaries

Would probably call it, a 'pulex vulgaris,')

When all at once,

With a rush and a bounce,

Who should appear but that same ameer,

His boots all mire,

And his riding attire

So shockingly damaged about the rear

That all the small street-boys kept asking him,

'whether

He was sure he'd not mislaid a good deal of leather?'

He straight drew forth the royal letter,

(A little bit creased and a trifle wetter

Than it was when the king his sign-manual august

Had affixed thereto,) and the envelope thrust

Under the nose of the wondering sage,

With little respect for his knowledge or age—

Merely said, 'Mind your eye!

Get up and be spry!

Put up a clean handkerchief and a white tie!

    Here's a horse all ready,

    Warranted steady;

Or, if you don't like him, why here's a nice Neddy!

I regret there was no time to bring you a cart,

    But please be smart:

Just five minutes, and then we must start!'

'Twas in vain that Muhammad Zákiria protested

That his last meal as yet was not quite digested;

That all his best garments were gone to the wash;

Et cetera.   The envoy said nothing but 'Bosh!'

And finding he wasn't inclined to hurry,

Without more demur, he

Called to his servants to come and surround him,

Who instantly floored him and carefully bound him,

Coolly carried him into the street,

And tied him on to a charger fleet;

Then they started away, like the desert wind,

And soon left the town of Rei leagues behind!

'T is needless the tale of their journey to tell—

How sometimes they stumbled, and sometimes they

 fell ;

What rivers they swam in the course of their ride,

And how often the doctor was wetted and dried ;

 But let us suppose

Them arrived at the court, where a change of clothes,

A large dose of liquor, a little repose,

A plentiful meal, and an upright position,

Made quite a new man of the learned physician !

 When he was shown

 To the foot of the throne,

His majesty said, in a gracious tone,

 ' How are you?

 How does your mother do ?

Your grandmother, uncle and aunt, and the other too?'

He uttered, in short, what, in every respect,

Oriental good-breeding considers correct :

 Then added, ' You know,

 I'm a good deal so so,

And the doctors about here are not worth a blow;

So much to my sorrow, to save time and money,

I was really obliged to waive all ceremony,

And send an ameer, in a friendly way,

To get you to come here and make a short stay;

    I trust you don't feel

    Any worse for the zeal

You've displayed in thus hurrying to soothe and to

    heal;

'T was done, pray remember, " pro aris et focis;"

    That is, for *me;*

    And now let us see

What 's the result of your diagnosis ?'

Muhammad Zákiria had looked meanwhile

At the king, and had reckoned the phlegm and the

    bile

And the humours and matters within that were

    seething,

By merely observing his manner of breathing;

So he answered at once with a bow and a smile,

' Your majesty's person 's been bothered enough

  With drugs and decoctions and that sort of stuff.

      There 's a certain—a—a—

      What shall I say ?—

A kind of " Je ne sais quoi" and a " bonhommie "

Perceptible in your august physiognomy,

That makes me think—seeing your—hum !—and the

    rest,

That a mental treatment will be the best !

      You will please to deign

      Just to remain

Perfectly quiet and tranquil a day or two,

While I remove, extirpate, and purge away a few

Trifling vapours that seem to retain

A hold on the liver, the lungs, and the brain !'

Having uttered these sapient observations,

He proceeded at once to operations,

And the royal stomach did straightway fill

With that wondrous specific, the ' real bread pill,'

Prescribing also every quarter

Of an hour, a good jorum of salt and water;

Then, after the lapse of a day or two,

He informed the patient, he 'thought he would
    do,'

And safely might now a new course pursue.

He then told the servants to go and see

That a big tub of water, as hot as could be,

Was prepared in his majesty's sanctum sanctorum,

With balms and sweet essences, 'more majorum;'

And he bade that a horse should his coming
    await,

All saddled and bridled, before the gate,

As he'd have to depart upon matters of state.

    Soon the king, with a sheet

On his royal back, in the steam and the heat,

Was fuming and fretting, and boiling and sweating,

And kicking and plunging, and constantly letting

o

Off volleys of various exclamations,

Appeals to the Prophet, and strong imprecations;

When lo and behold, with a threatening eye,

And a gleaming sabre lifted high,

There walked in Muhammad Zákiria of Rei !

Said he : ' Now, you wretched, mean, monkey-like
     thing,

Whom ignorant donkeys and idiots call " king !"

('Though if they had sense to become of my
     mind,

'Stead of bowing before, they would kick you be-
     hind !)

I've got you alone for a little while,

When there's no need to talk about " humours " and
     " bile,"

When I don't care the least if you frown or you
     smile ;

But intend to converse in my usual style.

And first, let me tell you, you're no king at all,

But only the chief of a poor, worn-out, small

Principality, now for some years the prey

Of whoever can take it, be he who he may.

Next, were you ten thousand times sultan and king,

Your glory, at best, is a very slight thing !

Let 's suppose you denuded of land and of power,

With no palace to shield you from sunshine or
    shower ;

    With no bowing and scraping

      Of nobles and flunkeys,

    Who keep constantly aping

      The actions of monkeys ;

With none of those trappings, for apes only fit,

In which you are daily accustomed to sit ;

In fact to be just as you squat there, a creature

Possessing no virtue, no single good feature ;

What do you think would be your price?

In the market you'd not fetch a single pice !

    Yet you have the cheek

    To send and seek

For me, who have studied both Hebrew and
    Greek ;
    Who, though I look meek,
    And gently speak,
Am a master of knowledge, that never is weak.

You send a big, thick-headed, frowsy ameer,

To bring me, "vi et armis" here ;

Who gives me no time to swallow a morsel,

But treats me just like a box or a parcel,

And without saying "By your leave," ties me by
    force

On an ugly, stumbling, beast of a horse,

And tugs me here through the mud and dirt.

And then you, forsooth, "hope I have not been
    hurt !"

All this is a little too much to bear,
    So I think that ere

I depart from this country, whose people and
    air

Are the most infernal I 've known anywhere,

I might venture upon such a trifling lark as
To let the life out of your useless carcase !'
    Just at that word
He rushed at the king, made a sweep with his
    sword,
Then ran through the door, which stood open wide,
Locked it and bolted it on the outside,
    Passed to the gate
    Where the steed did await,
In a moment the reins from the post untied,
Jumped on his back, and away did ride !

But now it is curious
    To tell
    What befell
The king, who had been made both funky and
    furious ;
At first he did nothing but rave and roar,
    Cursed and swore
Till his tongue was swelled and his throat was sore ;

Bid them follow, pursue,

    Cut the doctor in two,

Make him into a roast, and a hash, and a stew ;

But finding that nothing at all would do,

Dropped down and indulged in a regular boo-hoo !

After shedding a good many gallons of tears,

    He next, it appears,

Broke out in a copious perspiration,

While anger brought on ' healthy inflammation ;'

The aches and the cramps left his limbs and his
    joints ;

    And, thanks to his rage

    At the wily sage,

He soon became perfectly well at all points !

Muhammad Zákiria took very good care

To make no particular stay anywhere

Until he arrived at a place where the air

Was not breathed by subjects of Mansoor bin
 Nuh ;
And though the king sent several letters him to,
Chock-full of thanks, and describing his cure, ·
 And seeking the doctor again to allure,
  It was all of no use ;
 He knew that the great don't forget abuse ;
 And in his one answer, his majesty cravéd
To read the short story of Shimei and David.
Then, by way of a postscript, quoted a poet,
Who had written to this effect—' Not if I know it.'

LONDON : PRINTED BY
SPOTTISWOODE AND CO., NEW-STREET SQUARE
AND PARLIAMENT STREET

www.ingramcontent.com/pod-product-compliance
Lightning Source LLC
Chambersburg PA
CBHW020621030726
47497CB00007B/2351